CONFESSIONS

OF

A

MASK

By Yukio Mishima

TRANSLATED BY MEREDITH WEATHERBY

A NEW DIRECTIONS BOOK

. . . Beauty is a terrible and awful thing! It is terrible because it never has and never can be fathomed, for God sets us nothing but riddles. Within beauty both shores meet and all contradictions exist side by side. I'm not a cultivated man, brother, but I've thought a lot about this. Truly there are mysteries without end! Too many riddles weigh man down on earth. We guess them as we can, and come out of the water dry. Beauty! I cannot bear the thought that a man of noble heart and lofty mind sets out with the ideal of the Madonna and ends with the ideal of Sodom. What's still more awful is that the man with the ideal of Sodom in his soul does not renounce the ideal of the Madonna, and in the bottom of his heart he may still be on fire, sincerely on fire, with longing for the beautiful ideal, just as in the days of his youthful innocence. Yes, man's heart is wide, too wide indeed. I'd have it narrower. The devil only knows what to make of it! but what the intellect regards as shameful often appears splendidly beautiful to the heart. Is there beauty in Sodom? Believe me, most men find their beauty in Sodom. Did you know this secret? The dreadful thing is that beauty is not only terrifying but also mysterious. God and the Devil are fighting there, and their battlefield is the heart of man. But a man's heart wants to speak only of its own ache. Listen, now I'll tell you what it says. . . .

Dostoevski, THE BROTHERS KARAMAZOV

ISBN-13: 978-0-8112-0118-6

ISBN-10: 0-8112-0118-X

Originally entitled *Kamen No Kokuhaku*
Design by Stefan Salter
Manufactured in the United States of America
New Directions Books are published for James Laughlin
by New Directions Publishing Corporation,
80 Eighth Avenue, New York 10011.

CHAPTER ONE

For many years I claimed I could remember things seen at the time of my own birth. Whenever I said so, the grownups would laugh at first, but then, wondering if they were not being tricked, they would look distastefully at the pallid face of that unchildlike child. Sometimes I happened to say so in the presence of callers who were not close friends of the family; then my grandmother, fearing I would be taken for an idiot, would interrupt in a sharp voice and tell me to go somewhere else and play.

While they were still smiling from their laughter, the grownups would usually set about trying to confute me with some sort of scientific explanation. Trying to devise explanations that a child's mind could grasp, they would always start babbling with no little dramatic zeal, saying that a baby's eyes are not yet open at birth, or that even if his eyes are completely open, a newborn baby could not possibly see things clearly enough to remember them.

"Isn't that right?" they would say, shaking the small shoulder of the still-unconvinced child. But just then they would seem to be struck by the idea that they were on the point of being taken in by the child's tricks: Even if we think he's a child, we mustn't let our guard down. The little rascal is surely trying to trick us into telling him about "that," and then what is to keep him from asking, with still more childlike innocence: "Where did I come from? How was I born?" And in the end they would look me over again, silently, with a thin smile frozen on their lips, showing that for some reason, which I could never understand, their feelings had been deeply hurt.

But their fears were groundless. I had not the slightest desire to ask about "that." Even if I had wanted to ask, I was so fearful of hurting adult feelings that the thought of using trickery would never have occurred to me.

No matter how they explained, no matter how they laughed me away, I could not but believe I remembered my own birth. Perhaps the basis for my memory was something I had heard from someone who had been present at the time, or perhaps it was only my own willful imagination. However that may have been, there was one thing I was convinced I had seen clearly, with my own eyes. That was the brim of the basin in which I received my first bath. It was a brand-new basin, its wooden surface planed to a fresh and silken smoothness; and when I looked from inside, a ray of light was striking one spot on its brim. The wood gleamed only in that one spot and seemed to be made of gold. Tongue-tips of water lapped up waveringly as though they would lick the spot, but never quite reached it. And, whether because of a reflection or because the ray of light streamed on into the basin as well, the water beneath that spot on the brim gleamed softly, and tiny shining waves seemed to be forever bumping their heads together there. . . .

The strongest disproof of this memory was the fact that I had been born, not in the daytime, but at nine in the evening: There could have been no streaming sunlight. Even though teased with a "So then, it must have been an electric light," without any great difficulty I could still walk into the absurdity of believing that no matter if it had been midnight, a ray of sunlight had surely been striking at least that one spot on the basin. In this way the brim of that basin and its flickering light lingered on in my memory as something I had surely seen at the time of my first bath.

I was born two years after the Great Earthquake. Ten years earlier, as a result of a scandal that occurred while he was serving as a colonial governor, my grandfather had taken the blame for a subordinate's misdeeds and resigned his post. (I am not speaking euphemistically: until now I have never seen such a totality of foolish trust in human beings as that my grandfather possessed.) Thereafter my family had begun sliding down an incline with a speed so happy-go-lucky that I could almost say they hummed merrily as they went—huge debts, foreclosure, sale of the family estate, and then, as financial difficulties multiplied, a morbid vanity blazing higher and higher like some evil impulse. . . .

As a result I was born in not too good a section of Tokyo, in an old rented house. It was a pretentious house on a corner, with a rather jumbled appearance and a dingy, charred feeling. It had an imposing iron gate, an entry garden, and a Western-style reception room as large as the interior of a suburban church. There were two stories on the upper slope and three on the lower, numerous gloomy rooms, and six housemaids. In this house, which creaked like an old chest of drawers, ten persons were getting up and lying down morning and evening—my grandfather and grandmother, father and mother, and the servants.

At the root of the family troubles was my grandfather's passion for enterprises and my grandmother's illness and extravagant ways. My grandfather, tempted by the schemes that dubious cronies came bringing, often went traveling to distant places, dreaming dreams of gold. My grandmother came of an old family; she hated and scorned my grandfather. Hers was a narrow-minded, indomitable, and rather wildly poetic spirit. A chronic case of cranial neuralgia was indirectly but steadily gnawing away her nerves and at the same time adding an unavailing sharpness to her intellect. Who knows but what those fits of depression she continued having until her death were a memento of vices in which my grandfather had indulged in his prime?

Into this house my father had brought my mother, a frail and beautiful bride.

On the morning of January 4, 1925, my mother was attacked by labor pains. At nine that evening she gave birth to a small baby weighing five pounds and six ounces.

On the evening of the seventh day the infant was clothed in undergarments of flannel and cream-colored silk and a kimono of silk crepe with a splashed pattern. In the presence of the assembled household my grandfather drew my name on a strip of ceremonial paper and placed it on an offertory stand in the tokonoma.

My hair was blondish for a long time, but they kept putting olive oil on it until it finally turned black.

My parents lived on the second floor of the house. On the pretext that it was hazardous to raise a child on an upper floor, my grandmother snatched me from my mother's arms on my forty-ninth day. My bed was placed in my grandmother's sickroom, perpetually closed and stifling with odors of sickness and old age, and I was raised there beside her sickbed.

When about one year old I fell from the third step of the stairway and injured my forehead. My grandmother had gone to the theater, and my father's cousins and my mother were noisily enjoying the respite. My mother had had occasion to take something up to the second floor. Following her, I had become entangled in the trailing skirt of her kimono and had fallen.

My grandmother was summoned by telephone from the Kabuki Theater. When she arrived, my grandfather went out to meet her. She stood in the entryway without taking her shoes off, leaning on the cane that she carried in her right hand, and stared fixedly at my grandfather. When she spoke, it was in a strangely calm tone of voice, as though carving out each word:

"Is he dead?"

"No."

Then, taking off her shoes and stepping up from the entryway, she walked down the corridor with steps as confident as those of a priestess. . . .

On the New Year's morning just prior to my fourth birthday I vomited something the color of coffee. The family doctor was called. After examining me, he said he was not sure I would recover. I was given injections of camphor and glucose until I was like a pincushion. The pulses of both my wrist and upper arm became imperceptible.

Two hours passed. They stood looking down at my corpse.

A shroud was made ready, my favorite toys collected, and all the relatives gathered. Almost another hour passed, and then suddenly urine appeared. My mother's brother, who was a doctor, said, "He's alive!" He said it showed that the heart had resumed beating.

A little later urine appeared again. Gradually the vague light of life revived in my cheeks.

That illness—autointoxication—became chronic with me. It struck about once a month, now lightly, now seriously. I encountered many crises. By the sound of the disease's footsteps as it drew near I came to be able to sense whether an attack was likely to approach death or not.

My earliest memory, an unquestionable one, haunting me with a strangely vivid image, dates from about that time.

I do not know whether it was my mother, a nurse, a maid, or an aunt who was leading me by the hand. Nor is the season of the year distinct. Afternoon sunshine was falling dimly on the houses along the slope. Led by the hand of the unremembered woman, I was climbing the slope toward home. Someone was coming down the slope, and the woman jerked my hand. We got out of the way and stood waiting at one side.

There is no doubt that the image of what I saw then

has taken on meaning anew each of the countless times it has been reviewed, intensified, focused upon. Because within the hazy perimeter of the scene nothing but the figure of that "someone coming down the slope" stands out with disproportionate clarity. And not without reason: this very image is the earliest of those that have kept tormenting and frightening me all my life.

It was a young man who was coming down toward us, with handsome, ruddy cheeks and shining eyes, wearing a dirty roll of cloth around his head for a sweatband. He came down the slope carrying a yoke of night-soil buckets over one shoulder, balancing their heaviness expertly with his footsteps. He was a night-soil man, a ladler of excrement. He was dressed as a laborer, wearing split-toed shoes with rubber soles and black-canvas tops, and dark-blue cotton trousers of the close-fitting kind called "thigh-pullers."

The scrutiny I gave the youth was unusually close for a child of four. Although I did not clearly perceive it at the time, for me he represented my first revelation of a certain power, my first summons by a certain strange and secret voice. It is significant that this was first manifested to me in the form of a night-soil man: excrement is a symbol for the earth, and it was doubtlessly the malevolent love of the Earth Mother that was calling to me.

I had a presentiment then that there is in this world a kind of desire like stinging pain. Looking up at that

8

dirty youth, I was choked by desire, thinking, "I want to change into him," thinking, "I want to *be* him." I can remember clearly that my desire had two focal points. The first was his dark-blue "thigh-pullers," the other his occupation. The close-fitting jeans plainly outlined the lower half of his body, which moved lithely and seemed to be walking directly toward me. An inexpressible adoration for those trousers was born in me. I did not understand why.

His occupation . . . At that instant, in the same way that other children, as soon as they attain the faculty of memory, want to become generals, I became possessed with the ambition to become a night-soil man. The origin of this ambition might have been partly in the dark-blue jeans, but certainly not exclusively so. In time this ambition became still stronger and, expanding within me, saw a strange development.

What I mean is that toward his occupation I felt something like a yearning for a piercing sorrow, a body-wrenching sorrow. His occupation gave me the feeling of "tragedy" in the most sensuous meaning of the word. A certain feeling as it were of "self-renunciation," a certain feeling of indifference, a certain feeling of intimacy with danger, a feeling like a remarkable mixture of nothingness and vital power—all these feelings swarmed forth from his calling, bore down upon me, and took me captive, at the age of four. Probably I had a misconception of the work of a night-soil man.

Probably I had been told of some different occupation and, misled by his costume, was forcibly fitting his job into the pattern of what I had heard. I cannot otherwise explain it.

Such must have been the case because presently my ambition was transferred with those same emotions to the operators of hana-densha—those streetcars decorated so gaily with flowers for festival days—or again to subway ticket-punchers. Both occupations gave me a strong impression of "tragic lives" of which I was ignorant and from which it seemed I was forever excluded. This was particularly true in the case of the ticket-punchers: the rows of gold buttons on the tunics of their blue uniforms became fused in my mind with the odor which floated through the subways in those days—it was like the smell of rubber, or of peppermint —and readily called up mental associations of "tragic things." I somehow felt it was "tragic" for a person to make his living in the midst of such an odor. Existences and events occurring without any relationship to myself, occurring at places that not only appealed to my senses but were moreover denied to me—these, together with the people involved in them, constituted my definition of "tragic things." It seemed that my grief at being eternally excluded was always transformed in my dreaming into grief for those persons and their ways of life, and that solely through my own grief I was trying to share in their existences.

If such were the case, the so-called "tragic things" of which I was becoming aware were probably only shadows cast by a flashing presentiment of grief still greater in the future, of a lonelier exclusion still to come. . . .

There is another early memory, involving a picture book. Although I learned to read and write when I was five, I could not yet read the words in the book. So this memory also must date from the age of four.

I had several picture books about that time, but my fancy was captured, completely and exclusively, only by this one—and only by one eye-opening picture in it. I could dream away long and boring afternoons gazing at it, and yet when anyone came along, I would feel guilty without reason and would turn in a flurry to a different page. The watchfulness of a sicknurse or a maid vexed me beyond endurance. I longed for a life that would allow me to gaze at that picture all the day through. Whenever I turned to that page my heart beat fast. No other page meant anything to me.

The picture showed a knight mounted on a white horse, holding a sword aloft. The horse, nostrils flaring, was pawing the ground with powerful forelegs. There was a beautiful coat of arms on the silver armor the knight was wearing. The knight's beautiful face peeped through the visor, and he brandished his drawn sword awesomely in the blue sky, confronting either Death or, at the very least, some hurtling object full of evil power. I believed he would be killed the next instant: if I turn the page quickly, surely I can see him being killed. Surely there is some arrangement whereby, before one knows it, the pictures in a picture book can be changed into "the next instant." . . .

But one day my sicknurse happened to open the book to that page. While I was stealing a quick sideways glance at it, she said:

"Does little master know this picture's story?"

"No, I don't."

"This looks like a man, but it's a woman. Honestly. Her name was Joan of Arc. The story is that she went to war wearing a man's clothes and served her country."

"A woman . . . ?"

I felt as though I had been knocked flat. The person I had thought a *he* was a *she*. If this beautiful knight was a woman and not a man, what was there left? (Even today I feel a repugnance, deep rooted and hard to explain, toward women in male attire.) This was the first "revenge by reality" that I had met in life, and it seemed a cruel one, particularly upon the sweet fantasies I had cherished concerning *his* death. From that day on I turned my back on that picture book. I would never so much as take it in my hands again. Years later I was to discover a glorification of the death of a beautiful knight in a verse by Oscar Wilde:

Fair is the knight who lieth slain
Amid the rush and reed....

In his novel *Là-Bas,* Huysmans discusses the character of Gilles de Rais, bodyguard to Joan of Arc by royal command of Charles VII, saying that even though soon to be perverted to "the most sophisticated of cruelties, the most exquisite of crimes," the original impulse for his mysticism came from seeing with his own eyes all manner of miraculous deeds performed by Joan of Arc. Although she had a contrary effect upon me, arousing in me a feeling of repugnance, in my case also the Maid of Orleans played an important role. . . .

Yet another memory: It is the odor of sweat, an odor that drove me onward, awakened my longings, overpowered me. . . .

Pricking up my ears, I hear a crunching sound, muffled and very faint, seeming to menace. Once in a while a bugle joins in. A simple and strangely plaintive sound of singing approaches. Tugging at a maid's hand, I urge her to hurry hurry, wild to be standing at the gate, clasped in her arms.

It was the troops passing our gate as they returned from drill. Soldiers are fond of children, and I always looked forward to receiving some empty cartridges from them. As my grandmother had forbidden me to accept these gifts, saying they were dangerous, my anticipation was whetted by the joys of stealth. The heavy thudding of army shoes, stained uniforms, and a forest of shouldered rifles are enough to fascinate any child utterly. But it was simply their sweaty odor that fascinated me, forming a stimulus that lay concealed beneath my hope of receiving cartridges from them.

The soldiers' odor of sweat—that odor like a sea breeze, like the air, burned to gold, above the seashore —struck my nostrils and intoxicated me. This was probably my earliest memory of odors. Needless to say, the odor could not, at that time, have had any direct relationship with sexual sensations, but it did gradually and tenaciously arouse within me a sensuous craving for such things as the destiny of soldiers, the tragic nature of their calling, the distant countries they would see, the ways they would die. . . .

These odd images were the first things I encountered in life. From the beginning they stood before me in truly masterful completeness. There was not a single thing lacking. In later years I sought in them for the wellsprings of my own feelings and actions, and again not a single thing was lacking.

Ever since childhood my ideas concerning human existence have never once deviated from the Augustinian theory of predetermination. Over and over again I was tormented by vain doubts—even as I continue being tormented today—but I regarded such doubts as only another sort of temptation to sin, and remained unshaken in my deterministic views. I had been handed what might be called a full menu of all the troubles in my life while still too young to read it. But all I had to do was spread my napkin and face the table. Even the fact that I would now be writing an odd book like this was precisely noted on the menu, where it must have been before my eyes from the beginning.

The period of childhood is a stage on which time and space become entangled. For example, there was the news I heard from adults concerning events in various countries—the eruption of a volcano, say, or the insurrection of an army—and the things that were happening before my eyes—my grandmother's spells or the petty family quarrels—and the fanciful events of the fairy-tale world in which I had just then become immersed: these three things always appeared to me to be of equal value and like kind. I could not believe that the world was any more complicated than a structure of building blocks, nor that the so-called "social community," which I must presently enter, could be more dazzling than the world of fairy tales. Thus, without my being aware of it, one of the determinants of my life had come into operation. And because of my struggles against it, from the beginning my every fantasy was tinged with despair, strangely complete and in itself resembling passionate desire.

One night from my bed I saw a shining city floating upon the expanse of darkness that surrounded me. It was strangely still, and yet overflowed with brilliance and mystery. I could plainly see a mystic brand that had been impressed upon the faces of the persons in that city. They were adults, returning home in dead of night, still retaining in speech or gesture traces of something like secret signs and countersigns, something smacking of Freemasonry. Moreover, in their faces there shone a glistening fatigue that made them shy of being looked at full in the face. As with those holiday masks that leave powdered silver on the fingertips when one touches them, it seemed that if I could but touch their faces, I might discover the color of the pigments with which the city of night had painted them.

Presently Night raised a curtain directly before my eyes, revealing the stage on which Shokyokusai Tenkatsu performed her feats of magic. (She was then making one of her rare appearances at a theater in the Shinjuku district; although the staging of the magician Dante, whom I saw at the same theater some years later, was on a many times grander scale than hers, neither Dante nor even the Universal Exhibition of the Hagenbeck Circus amazed me so much as my first view of Tenkatsu.)

She lounged indolently about the stage, her opulent body veiled in garments like those of the Great Harlot of the Apocalypse. On her arms were flashy bracelets, heaped with artificial stones; her make-up was as heavy as that of a female ballad-singer, with a coating of white powder extending even to the tips of her toenails; and she wore a trumpery costume that surrendered her person over to the kind of brazen luster given off only by shoddy merchandise. And yet, curiously enough, all this somehow achieved a melancholy harmony with her haughty air of self-importance, characteristic of conjurers and exiled noblemen alike, with her sort of somber charm, with her heroine-like bearing. The delicate grain of the shadow cast by these unharmonious elements produced its own surprising and unique illusion of harmony.

I understood, though vaguely, that the desire "to become Tenkatsu" and "to become a streetcar operator" differed in essence. Their most marked dissimilarity was the fact that in the case of Tenkatsu the craving for that "tragic quality" was almost wholly lacking. In wishing to become Tenkatsu I did not have to taste that bitter mixture of longing and shame. And yet one day, trying hard to still my heartbeats, I stole into my mother's room and opened the drawers of her clothing chest.

From among my mother's kimonos I dragged out the most gorgeous one, the one with the strongest colors. For a sash I chose an obi on which scarlet roses were painted in oil, and wrapped it round and round my waist in the manner of a Turkish pasha. I covered my head with a wrapping-cloth of crepe de Chine. My cheeks flushed with wild delight when I stood before the mirror and saw that this improvised headcloth resembled those of the pirates in *Treasure Island*.

But my work was still far from complete. My every point, down to the very tips of my fingernails, had to be made worthy of the creation of mystery. I stuck a hand mirror in my sash and powdered my face lightly. Then I armed myself with a silver-colored flashlight, an old-fashioned fountain pen of chased metal, and whatever else struck my eye.

I assumed a solemn air and, dressed like this, rushed into my grandmother's sitting-room. Unable to suppress my frantic laughter and delight, I ran about the room crying:

"I'm Tenkatsu! Me, I'm Tenkatsu!"

My grandmother was there sick abed, and also my mother and a visitor and the maid assigned to the sickroom. But not a single person was visible to my eyes. My frenzy was focused upon the consciousness that, through my impersonation, Tenkatsu was being revealed to many eyes. In short, I could see nothing but myself.

And then I chanced to catch sight of my mother's face. She had turned slightly pale and was simply sitting there as though absent-minded. Our glances met; she lowered her eyes.

I understood. Tears blurred my eyes.

What was it I understood at that moment, or was on the verge of understanding? Did the motif of later years—that of "remorse as prelude to sin"—show here the first hint of its beginning? Or was the moment teaching me how grotesque my isolation would appear to the eyes of love, and at the same time was I learning, from the reverse side of the lesson, my own incapacity for accepting love? . . .

The maid grabbed me and took me to another room. In an instant, just as though I were a chicken for plucking, she had me stripped of my outrageous masquerade.

My passion for such dressing-up was aggravated when I began going to movies. It continued markedly until I was about nine.

Once I went with our student houseboy to see a film version of the operetta *Fra Diavolo*. The character playing Diavolo wore an unforgettable court costume with cascades of lace at the wrists. When I said how much I should like to dress like that and wear such a wig, the student laughed derisively. And yet I knew that in the servant quarters he often amused the maids with his imitations of the Kabuki character Princess Yaegaki.

After Tenkatsu there came Cleopatra to fascinate me. Once on a snowy day toward the end of December a friendly doctor, yielding to my entreaties, took me to see a movie about her. As it was the end of the year, the audience was small. The doctor put his feet up on the railing and fell asleep. All alone I gazed avidly, completely enchanted: The Queen of Egypt making her entry into Rome, borne aloft on an ancient and curiously wrought litter carried on the shoulders of a multitude of slaves. Melancholy eyes, the lids thickly stained with eye-shadow. Her other-worldly apparel. And then, later, her half-naked, amber-colored body coming into view from out the Persian rug. . . .

This time, already taking thorough delight in misconduct, I eluded the eyes of my grandmother and parents and, with my younger sister and brother as accomplices, devoted myself to dressing up as Cleopatra. What was I hoping for from this feminine attire? It was not until much later that I discovered hopes the same as mine in Heliogabalus, emperor of Rome in its period of decay, that destroyer of Rome's ancient gods, that decadent, bestial monarch.

The night-soil man, the Maid of Orleans, and the soldiers' sweaty odor formed one sort of preamble to my life. Tenkatsu and Cleopatra were a second. There is yet a third that should be related.

Although as a child I read every fairy story I could lay my hands on, I never liked the princesses. I was fond only of the princes. I was all the fonder of princes murdered or princes fated for death. I was completely in love with any youth who was killed.

But I did not yet understand why, from among Andersen's many fairy tales, only his "Rose-Elf" threw deep shadows over my heart, only that beautiful youth who, while kissing the rose given him as a token by his sweetheart, was stabbed to death and decapitated by a villain with a big knife. I did not yet understand why, out of Wilde's numerous fairy tales, it was only the corpse of the young fisherman in "The Fisherman and His Soul," washed up on the shore clasping a mermaid to his breast, that captivated me.

Naturally I was also fond enough of other childlike things. There was Andersen's "The Nightingale," which I liked well, and I delighted in many childish comic books. But my heart's leaning toward Death and Night and Blood would not be denied.

Visions of "princes slain" pursued me tenaciously. Who could have explained for me why I was so delighted with fancies in which those body-revealing tights worn by the princes were associated with their cruel deaths? There is a Hungarian fairy tale that I particularly remember in this connection. For a long time my heart was captivated by an extremely realistic illustration to this story.

Printed in primary colors, the illustration showed the prince dressed in black tights and a rose-colored tunic with spun-gold embroidery on the breast. A dark-blue cape that flashed a scarlet lining was flung about his shoulders, and around his waist there was a green and gold belt. He was equipped with a helmet of green gold, a bright-red sword, and a quiver of green leather. His left hand, gloved in white leather, grasped a bow; his right hand rested upon the branch of one of the ancient trees of the forest; and with a grave, commanding countenance he was looking down the terrifying throat of the raging dragon that was about to set upon him. On his face was the resolve of death. If this prince had been destined to be a conqueror in his engagement with the dragon, how faint would have been his fascination for me. But fortunately the prince was destined to die.

To my regret, however, his fate of death was not perfect. In order to rescue his sister and also to marry a beautiful princess, seven times did this prince endure the ordeal of death and, thanks to the magical powers of a diamond that he held in his mouth, seven times did he rise from death, finally living happily ever after.

The illustration showed a scene just prior to death number one—being devoured by a dragon. After that he was "caught by a great spider and, after his body had been shot full of poison, was eaten ravenously." Again, he was drowned, roasted in a fire, stung by hornets and bitten by snakes, flung bodily into a pit completely lined with there is no saying how many great knives planted with their points up, and crushed to death by countless boulders that came falling "like a torrential rain."

His death by being devoured by the dragon was described in particular detail:

"Without a moment's delay, the dragon chewed the prince greedily into bits. It was almost more than he could stand, but the prince summoned all his courage and bore the torture steadfastly until he was finally chewed completely into shreds. Then, in a flash, he *suddenly was put back together again and came springing nimbly right out of the dragon's mouth. There was not a single scratch anywhere on his body. The dragon* sank to the ground and died on the spot."

I read this passage hundreds of times. But the sentence "There was not a single scratch anywhere on his body" seemed to me to be a defect that could not go unchallenged. Reading this, I felt the author had both betrayed me and committed a grave error.

Before long I chanced upon a discovery. This was to read the passage while hiding under my hand: *suddenly was put back together again and came springing nimbly right out of the dragon's mouth. There was not a single scratch anywhere on his body. The dragon.* Thereupon the story became ideal:

"Without a moment's delay, the dragon chewed the prince greedily into bits. It was almost more than he could stand, but the prince summoned all his courage and bore the torture steadfastly until he was finally chewed completely into shreds. Then, in a flash, he sank to the ground and died on the spot."

An adult would certainly have seen the absurdity in such a method of cutting. And even that young and arrogant censor discerned the patent contradiction between "being chewed completely into shreds" and "sinking to the ground," but he was easily infatuated with his own fancies and found it still impossible to discard either phrase.

On the other hand, I delighted in imagining situations in which I myself was dying in battle or being murdered. And yet I had an abnormally strong fear of death. One day I would bully a maid to tears, and the next morning I would see her serving breakfast with a cheerfully smiling face, as though nothing had happened. Then I would read all manner of evil meanings into her smiles. I could not believe them to be other than the diabolical smiles that come from being fully confident of victory. I was sure she was plotting to poison me out of revenge. Waves of fear billowed up in my breast. I was positive the poison had been put in my bowl of broth, and I would not have touched it for all the world. I ended many such meals by jumping up from the table and staring hard at the maid, as though to say "So there!" It seemed to me that the woman was so dismayed at this thwarting of her plans for poisoning me that she could not rise, but was only staring from across the table at the broth, now become completely cold, with some dust floating on its surface, and telling herself I'd left too much for the poison to be effective.

Out of concern for my frail health and also to keep me from learning bad things, my grandmother had forbidden me to play with the neighborhood boys, and my only playmates, excepting maids and nurses, were three girls whom my grandmother had selected from the girls of the neighborhood. The slightest noise affected my grandmother's neuralgia—the violent opening or closing of a door, a toy bugle, wrestling, or any conspicuous sound or vibration whatsoever—and our playing had to be quieter than is usual even among girls. Rather than this I preferred by far to be by myself reading a book, playing with my building blocks, indulging in my willful fancies, or drawing pictures. When my sister and brother were born, they were not given over into my grandmother's hands as I had been, and my father saw to it that they were reared with a freedom befitting children. And yet I did not greatly envy them their liberty and rowdiness.

But things were different when I went visiting at the homes of my cousins. Then even I was called upon to be a boy, a male. An incident which should be related occurred in the early spring of my seventh year, shortly before I entered primary school, during a visit to the home of a certain cousin whom I shall call Sugiko. Upon our arrival there—my grandmother had accompanied me—my great-aunt had praised me to the skies —"How he's grown! How big he's become!"—and my grandmother had been so taken in by this flattery that she had granted a special dispensation regarding the meals I took there. Until then she had been so frightened by the frequent attacks of autointoxication I have already mentioned that she had forbidden me to eat all "blue-skinned" fish. My diet had been carefully limited: of fish, I was allowed only such white-flesh kinds as halibut, turbot, or red snapper; of potatoes, only those mashed and strained through a colander; of sweets, all bean-jams were forbidden and there were only light biscuits, wafers, and other such dry confections; and of fruits, only apples cut in thin slices, or small portions of mandarin oranges. Hence it was on this visit that I ate my first blue-skinned fish—a yellowtail—which I devoured with immense satisfaction. Its delicate flavor signified for me that I had finally been accorded the first of my adult rights, but at the same time it left a rather bitter tang of uneasiness upon the tip of my tongue—uneasiness at becoming an adult—which still recalls me to a feeling of discomfort whenever I taste that flavor.

Sugiko was a healthy girl, overflowing with life. I myself had never been able to go to sleep easily, and when staying at her house and lying in the same room on the pallet next to hers, I would watch with a mixture of envy and admiration how Sugiko always fell asleep instantly upon lowering her head to the pillow, exactly like a machine.

I had many times more freedom at Sugiko's house than at my own. As the imaginary enemies who must want to steal me away—my parents, in short—were not present, my grandmother had no qualms about giving me more liberty. There was no need to keep me always within reach of her eyes, as when at home.

And yet I was unable to take any great pleasure in this freedom that was allowed me. Like an invalid taking his first steps during convalescence, I had a feeling of stiffness as though I were acting under the compulsion of some imaginary obligation. I missed my bed of idleness. And in this house it was tacitly required that I act like a boy. The reluctant masquerade had begun. At about this time I was beginning to understand vaguely the mechanism of the fact that what people regarded as a pose on my part was actually an expression of my need to assert my true nature, and that it was precisely what people regarded as my true self which was a masquerade.

It was this unwilling masquerade that made me say:

"Let's play war."

As my companions were two girls—Sugiko and another cousin—playing at war was hardly a suitable game. Still less did the opposing Amazons show any signs of enthusiasm. My reason for proposing the game also lay in my inverted sense of social duty: in short, I felt that I must not fawn upon the girls, but must somehow give them a hard time.

Although mutually bored, we continued playing our clumsy game of war in and out of the twilit house.

From behind a bush Sugiko was imitating the sound of a machine gun:

"Bang! bang! bang!"

I finally decided it was about time to put an end to the business and led a wild flight into the house. The female soldiers came running after me, giving a continuous fusillade of bang-bang-bang's. I clutched at my heart and collapsed limply in the center of the parlor.

"What's the matter, Kochan?" they asked, approaching with worried faces.

"I'm being dead on the battlefield," I replied, neither opening my eyes nor moving my hand.

I was enraptured with the vision of my own form lying there, twisted and fallen. There was an unspeakable delight in having been shot and being on the point of death. It seemed to me that since it was I, even if actually struck by a bullet, there would surely be no pain. . . .

The years of childhood . . .

My memory runs head-on into a scene that is like a symbol of those years. To me as I am today, that scene represents childhood itself, past and irrecoverable. When I saw the scene I felt the hand of farewell with which childhood would take its leave of me. I had a premonition at that instant that all my feeling of subjective time, or timelessness, might one day gush forth from within me and flood into the mold of that scene, to become an exact imitation of its people and movements and sounds; that simultaneous with the completion of this copy, the original might melt away into the distant perspectives of real and objective time; and that I might be left with nothing more than the mere imitation or, to say it another way, with nothing more than an accurately stuffed specimen of my childhood.

Everyone experiences some such incident in his childhood. In most cases, however, it assumes such a slight form, hardly worthy of being called even an incident, that it is apt to pass by unnoticed. . . .

The scene of which I speak took place once when a crowd celebrating the Summer Festival came surging in through our gate.

Both for my sake and because of her bad leg, my grandmother had persuaded the neighborhood firemen to arrange for the festival processions of the district to pass along the street before our gate. Originally there had been another prescribed route for the festivals, but the chief fireman took it upon himself to arrange some slight detour each year, and it had become a custom to pass our house.

On this particular day I was standing in front of the gate with other members of the household. Both leaves of the vine-patterned iron gate had been thrown open, and water had been sprinkled neatly on the paving stones outside the gate. The hesitant sound of drums was drawing near.

The plaintive melody of a chant, in which individual words only gradually became distinguishable, pierced through the confused tumult of the festival, proclaiming what might be called the true theme of this outwardly purposeless uproar—a seeming lamentation for the extremely vulgar mating of humanity and eternity, which could be consummated only through some such pious immorality as this. In the tangled mass of sound I could gradually distinguish the metallic jingle of the rings on the staff carried by the priest at the head of the procession, the stuttering roar of the drums, and the medley of rhythmic shouts from the youths shouldering the sacred shrine. My heart was beating so suffocatingly that I could scarcely stand. (Ever since then violent anticipation has always been anguish rather than joy for me.)

The priest carrying the staff was wearing a fox mask. The golden eyes of this occult beast fastened themselves too intently upon me, as though to bewitch me, and the procession passing before my eyes aroused in me a joy akin to terror. Before I knew it, I felt myself grab hold of the skirt of whoever it was from our house that was standing beside me: I was ready to run away at the first excuse. (Ever since those days this has been the attitude with which I have always confronted life: from things too much waited for, too much embellished with anticipatory daydreams, there is in the end nothing I can do but run away.)

Behind the priest came a group of firemen, carrying on their shoulders the offertory chest, festooned with sacred garlands of twisted straw, and then a crowd of children carrying a tiny, frivolously bouncing shrine. Finally the principal shrine of the procession drew near, the majestic black and gold *omikoshi*. From afar we had already seen the golden phoenix on its peak, swaying and rocking dazzlingly above the din and bustle, like a bird floating to and fro among the waves; already the sight had filled us with a sort of bewildered feeling of uneasiness. Now the shrine itself came into view, and there was a venomous state of dead calm, like the air of the tropics, which clung solely about the shrine. It seemed a malevolent sluggishness, trembling hotly above the naked shoulders of the young men carrying the *omikoshi*. And within the thick scarlet-and-white ropes, within the guardrails of black lacquer and gold, behind those fast-shut doors of gold leaf, there was a four-foot cube of pitch-blackness.

This perfect cube of empty night, ceaselessly swaying and leaping, to and fro, up and down, was boldly reigning over the cloudless noonday of early summer.

The shrine drew closer and closer. The young men who carried it were wearing summer kimono, all of the same pattern, the thin cotton material revealing almost all their bodies, and their motions made it seem as though the shrine itself were staggering-drunk. Their legs seemed to be one great tangle, and it was as though

31

their eyes were not looking upon things of this earth. The young man who carried the great round fan of authority was running around the edges of the group, urging them on with wonderfully loud shouts. From time to time the shrine would tilt crazily. Then, with even more frenzied shouting, it would be recovered.

At this point—perhaps because the adults in my family had intuitively perceived that, although the young men seemed outwardly to be parading along just as before, there was some power in them that was demanding an outlet—I was suddenly shoved back by the hand of the person onto whom I had been clinging.

"Look out!" someone shouted.

I could not tell what happened after that. Pulled by the hand, I ran fleeing through the entry garden and dashed into the house through a side door.

I rushed up to the second floor with someone and out onto the balcony. From there I looked down upon the scene, breathlessly. Just at that moment they had come swarming into the entry garden, bearing their black shrine.

Even long after, I wondered what force impelled them to such an action. I still do not know. How could those scores of young men have suddenly arrived at the decision, instantaneous and single-minded, to come rushing in through our gate?

They took delight in wanton destruction of the plants. It was a rout in every sense of the word. The entry garden, which had long since been exhausted of all interest for me, was suddenly transformed into a different world. The shrine was paraded over every inch of it, and the shrubs, ripped apart crashingly, were trampled underfoot. It was difficult for me so much as to tell what was happening. The noises were neutralizing each other, and it seemed exactly as though my ears were being struck by recurrent waves of frozen silence and meaningless roaring. Likewise with the colors—gold and vermilion, purple and green, yellow and dark blue, all throbbed and boiled up and seemed like a single color in which now gold and now vermilion was the dominant hue.

Through it all there was only one vividly clear thing, a thing that both horrified and lacerated me, filling my heart with unaccountable agony. This was the expression on the faces of the young men carrying the shrine—an expression of the most obscene and undisguised drunkenness in the world. . . .

CHAPTER TWO

For over a year now I had been suffering the anguish of a child provided with a curious toy. I was twelve years old.

This toy increased in volume at every opportunity and hinted that, rightly used, it would be quite a delightful thing. But directions for its use were nowhere written, and so, when the toy took the initiative in wanting to play with me, my bewilderment was inevitable. Occasionally my humiliation and impatience became so aggravated that I even thought I wanted to destroy the toy. In the end, however, there was nothing for it but to surrender on my side to the insubordinate toy, with its expression of sweet secrecy, and wait passively to see what would happen.

Then I took it into my head to try listening more

dispassionately to the toy's wishes. When I did so, I found that soon it already possessed its own definite and unmistakable tastes, or what might be called its own mechanism. The nature of its tastes had become bound up, not only with my childhood memories, but, one after another, with such things as the naked bodies of young men seen on a summer's seashore, the swimming teams seen at Meiji Pool, the swarthy young man a cousin of mine married, and the valiant heroes of many an adventure story. Until then I had mistakenly thought I was only poetically attracted to such things, thus confusing the nature of my sensual desires with a system of esthetics.

The toy likewise raised its head toward death and pools of blood and muscular flesh. Gory dueling scenes on the frontispieces of adventure-story magazines, which I borrowed in secret from the student houseboy; pictures of young samurai cutting open their bellies, or of soldiers struck by bullets, clenching their teeth and dripping blood from between hands that clutched at khaki-clad breasts; photographs of hard-muscled sumo wrestlers, of the third rank and not yet grown too fat— at the sight of such things the toy would promptly lift its inquisitive head. (If the adjective "inquisitive" be inappropriate, it can be changed to read either "erotic" or "lustful.")

Coming to understand these matters, I began to seek physical pleasure consciously, intentionally. The principles of selection and arrangement were brought into operation. When the composition of a picture in an adventure-story magazine was found defective, I would first copy it with crayons, and then correct it to my satisfaction. Then it would become the picture of a young circus performer dropping to his knees and clutching at a bullet wound in his breast; or a tight-rope walker who had fallen and split his skull open and now lay dying, half his face covered with blood. Often at school I would become so preoccupied with the fear that these bloodthirsty pictures, which I had hidden away in a drawer of the bookcase at home, might be discovered during my absence that I would not even hear the teacher's voice. I knew I should have destroyed them promptly after drawing them, but my toy was so attached to them that I found it absolutely impossible to do so.

In this manner my insubordinate toy passed many futile days and months without achieving even its secondary goal—what I shall call my "bad habit"—let alone its ultimate, its primary goal.

Various changes had been taking place about me. The family had divided into two and, leaving the house where I was born, had moved into separate houses, not over half a block apart on the same street. My grandparents and I were in one house, while my parents and my sister and brother were in the other. During this time my father was sent abroad on official business, toured several countries in Europe, and returned home. Before long my parents moved again. My father had finally reached the belated resolve to reclaim me back into his own household and took this opportunity to do so. I underwent a scene of parting with my grandmother —"modern melodrama" my father called it—and thus finally went to live with my parents. Now I was separated from the house where my grandparents lived by several stops on the government railway and the municipal streetcar line. Day and night my grandmother clasped my photograph to her bosom, weeping, and was instantly seized with a paroxysm if I violated the treaty stipulation that I should come to spend one night each week with her. At the age of twelve I had a true-love sweetheart, aged sixty.

Presently my father was transferred to Osaka. He went alone, the rest of us remaining behind in Tokyo.

One day, taking advantage of having been kept from school by a slight cold, I got out some volumes of art reproductions, which my father had brought back as souvenirs of his foreign travels, and took them to my room, where I looked through them attentively. I was particularly enchanted by the photogravures of Grecian sculptures in the guidebooks to various Italian museums. When it came to depictions of the nude, among the many reproductions of masterpieces, it was these plates, in black and white, that best suited my fancy.

This was probably due to the simple fact that, even in reproductions, the sculpture seemed the more lifelike.

This was the first time I had seen these books. My miserly father, hating to have the pictures touched and stained by children's hands, and also fearing—how mistakenly!—that I might be attracted by the nude women of the masterpieces, had kept the books hidden away deep in the recesses of a cupboard. And for my part, until that day I had never dreamed they could be more interesting than the pictures in adventure-story magazines.

I began turning a page toward the end of a volume. Suddenly there came into view from one corner of the next page a picture that I had to believe had been lying in wait there for me, for my sake.

It was a reproduction of Guido Reni's "St. Sebastian," which hangs in the collection of the Palazzo Rosso at Genoa.

The black and slightly oblique trunk of the tree of execution was seen against a Titian-like background of gloomy forest and evening sky, somber and distant. A remarkably handsome youth was bound naked to the trunk of the tree. His crossed hands were raised high, and the thongs binding his wrists were tied to the tree. No other bonds were visible, and the only covering for the youth's nakedness was a coarse white cloth knotted loosely about his loins.

I guessed it must be a depiction of a Christian martyrdom. But, as it was painted by an esthetic painter of the eclectic school that derived from the Renaissance, even this painting of the death of a Christian saint has about it a strong flavor of paganism. The youth's body —it might even be likened to that of Antinous, beloved of Hadrian, whose beauty has been so often immortalized in sculpture—shows none of the traces of missionary hardship or decrepitude that are to be found in depictions of other saints; instead, there is only the springtime of youth, only light and beauty and pleasure.

His white and matchless nudity gleams against a background of dusk. His muscular arms, the arms of a praetorian guard accustomed to bending of bow and wielding of sword, are raised at a graceful angle, and his bound wrists are crossed directly over his head. His face is turned slightly upward and his eyes are open wide, gazing with profound tranquility upon the glory of heaven. It is not pain that hovers about his straining chest, his tense abdomen, his slightly contorted hips, but some flicker of melancholy pleasure like music. Were it not for the arrows with their shafts deeply sunk into his left armpit and right side, he would seem more a Roman athlete resting from fatigue, leaning against a dusky tree in a garden.

The arrows have eaten into the tense, fragrant, youthful flesh and are about to consume his body from within with flames of supreme agony and ecstasy. But there is no flowing blood, nor yet the host of arrows seen in other pictures of Sebastian's martyrdom. Instead, two lone arrows cast their tranquil and graceful shadows upon the smoothness of his skin, like the shadows of a bough falling upon a marble stairway.

But all these interpretations and observations came later.

That day, the instant I looked upon the picture, my entire being trembled with some pagan joy. My blood soared up; my loins swelled as though in wrath. The monstrous part of me that was on the point of bursting awaited my use of it with unprecedented ardor, up-braiding me for my ignorance, panting indignantly. My hands, completely unconsciously, began a motion they had never been taught. I felt a secret, radiant something rise swift-footed to the attack from inside me. Suddenly it burst forth, bringing with it a blinding intoxication. . . .

Some time passed, and then, with miserable feelings, I looked around the desk I was facing. A maple tree at the window was casting a bright reflection over every-thing—over the ink bottle, my schoolbooks and notes, the dictionary, the picture of St. Sebastian. There were cloudy-white splashes about—on the gold-imprinted title of a textbook, on a shoulder of the ink bottle, on one corner of the dictionary. Some objects were dripping lazily, leadenly, and others gleamed dully, like the eyes of a dead fish. Fortunately, a reflex motion of my hand to protect the picture had saved the book from being soiled.

This was my first ejaculation. It was also the beginning, clumsy and completely unpremeditated, of my "bad habit."

(It is an interesting coincidence that Hirschfeld should place "pictures of St. Sebastian" in the first rank of those kinds of art works in which the invert takes special delight. This observation of Hirschfeld's leads easily to the conjecture that in the overwhelming majority of cases of inversion, especially of congential inversion, the inverted and the sadistic impulses are inextricably entangled with each other.)

Tradition has it that St. Sebastian was born about the middle of the third century, became a captain in the Praetorian Guard of Rome, and ended his short life of thirty-odd years in martyrdom. He is said to have died in the year 288, during the reign of the Emperor Diocletian. Diocletian, a self-made man who had seen much of life, was admired for his benevolence. But Maximian, the coemperor, abhorred Christianity and condemned the Numidian youth Maximilianus to death for refusing, in the name of Christian pacifism, to perform the required military service. Marcellus the Centurion was likewise executed for this same religious constancy. This, then, is the historical background against which the martyrdom of St. Sebastian becomes understandable.

Sebastian became a secret convert to Christianity, used his position as captain in the Praetorian Guard to console the imprisoned Christians, and converted various Romans, including the mayor; when these activities became known, he was sentenced to death. He was shot with countless arrows and left for dead. But a pious widow, who came to bury him, discovered that his body was still warm, and nursed him back to life. Immediately, however, he defied the emperor, reviling the emperor's gods. This time he was beaten to death with clubs.

The broad outlines of this legend may well be true; certainly many such martyrdoms are known to have taken place. As for the suspicion that no human being could have been restored to life after receiving so many arrow wounds, may this not be a later embellishment, a familiar use of the resurrection theme in response to mankind's demand for miracles?

Desiring that my own rapture before the legend, before the picture, be understood more clearly as the fierce, sensual thing it was, I insert the following unfinished piece, which I wrote several years later:

St. Sebastian—A Prose Poem
Out of a schoolroom window once I spied a tree of middling height, swaying in the wind. As I looked,

my heart began to thunder. It was a tree of startling beauty. Upon the lawn it erected an upright triangle tinged with roundness; the heavy feeling of its verdure was supported on its many branches, thrusting upward and outward with the balanced symmetry of a candelabrum; and beneath the greenery there showed a sturdy trunk, like an ebony pedestal. There it stood, that tree, perfect, exquisitely wrought, but not losing any of Nature's grace and artlessness, keeping serene silence as though it itself were its own creator. And yet at the same time it assuredly was a created thing. Maybe a musical composition. A piece of chamber music by a German master. Music giving such religious, tranquil pleasure that it could only be called sacred, filled with the solemnity and longing found in the patterns of stately wall tapestries. . . .

And so the affinity between the shape of the tree and the sounds of music had some meaning for me. Little wonder then that when I was attacked by the two of them together, all the stronger in alliance, my indescribable, mysterious emotion should have been akin, not to lyricism, but to that sinsister intoxication found in the conjunction of religion and music.

Suddenly I asked in my heart: "Was this not the very tree—the tree to which the young saint was bound with his hands behind him, over the trunk of which his sacred blood trickled like driblets after a rain? that Roman tree on which he writhed, ablaze in a final agony

43

of death, with the harsh scraping of his young flesh against the bark as his final evidence of all earthly pleasure and pain?"

In the traditional annals of martyrdom it is said that, during the time following his enthronement when Diocletian was dreaming of power as limitless as the unobstructed soaring of a bird, there was a young captain of the Praetorian Guard who was seized and charged with the crime of serving a forbidden god. He was a young captain endowed both with a lithe body reminding one of the famous Oriental slave beloved by the Emperor Hadrian and with the eyes of a conspirator, as emotionless as the sea. He was charmingly arrogant. On his helmet he wore a white lily, presented to him each morning by maidens of the town. Drooping downward gracefully along the flow of his manly hair as he rested from fierce tourneying, the lily looked exactly like the nape of a swan's neck.

There was none who knew his place of birth, nor whence he came. But all who saw him felt this youth, with the physique of a slave and the features of a prince, to be a wayfarer who would soon be gone. To them it seemed that this Endymion was a nomad, leading his flocks; that this was the very person chosen to find a pasture darker green than other pastures.

Again, there were maidens who cherished the firm belief that he had come from the sea. Because within his breast could be heard the roaring of the sea. Because *in the pupils of his eyes there lingered the mysterious and eternal horizon that the sea leaves as a keepsake deep in the eyes of all who are born at the seaside and forced to depart from it. Because his sighs were sultry like the tidal breezes of full summer, fragrant with a smell of seaweed cast up upon the shore.*

This was Sebastian, young captain in the Praetorian Guard. And was not such beauty as his a thing destined for death? Did not the robust women of Rome, their senses nurtured on the taste of good wine that shook the bones and on the savor of meat dripping red with blood, quickly scent his ill-starred fate, as yet unknown to him, and love him for that reason? His blood was coursing with an even fiercer pace than usual within his white flesh, watching for an opening from which to spurt forth when that flesh would soon be torn asunder. How could the women have failed to hear the tempestuous desires of such blood as this?

His was not a fate to be pitied. In no way was it a pitiable fate. Rather was it proud and tragic, a fate that might even be called shining.

When one considers well, it seems likely that many a time, even in the midst of a sweet kiss, a foretaste of the agony of death must have furrowed his brow with a fleeting shadow of pain.

Also he must have foreseen, if dimly, that it was nothing less than martyrdom which lay in wait for him along the way; that this brand which Fate had set upon him was precisely the token of his apartness from all the ordinary men of earth.

Now, on that particular morning, Sebastian kicked off his covers and sprang from bed at break of day, pressed with martial duties. There was a dream he had dreamt at dawn—ill-omened magpies flocking in his breast, covering his mouth with flapping wings—and not yet had it vanished from his pillow. But the crude bed in which he lay himself down each night was shedding a fragrance of seaweed cast up upon the shore; surely then such perfume as this would lure him on for many a night to come to dreams of sea and wide horizons.

As he stood at the window and donned his creaking armor, he looked across the way at a temple surrounded by a grove, and in the skies above it he saw the sinking of the clustered stars called Mazzaroth. He looked at that magnificent pagan temple, and in the subtle arching of his eyebrows there came a look of deep contempt, akin almost to suffering and well becoming his beauty. Invoking the name of the only God, he softly chanted some awesome verses of the Holy Scriptures. And thereupon, as though the faintness of his chant were multiplied a thousandfold and echoed with majestic resonance, he heard a mighty moaning that came, there was no doubt, from that accursed temple, from those rows of columns partitioning the starry heavens. It was a sound like that of some strange cumulation crumbling into bits, resounding against the star-encrusted dome of sky.

He smiled and lowered his eyes to a point beneath his window. There was a group of maidens ascending secretly to his chambers for morning prayers, as was their custom in the darkness before each dawn. And in her hand each maiden bore a lily that still was sleeping closed. . . .

It was well into the winter of my second year in middle school. By then we had become accustomed to long trousers and to calling each other by unadorned surnames. (In lower school we had never been permitted to leave our knees bare below our short pants, not even at the height of summer, and thus our joy at first putting on long trousers had been doubled by the knowledge that never again would we have to garter our thighs painfully. In lower school we had also had to use the formal form of address when calling each other by name.) We had become accustomed as well to the splendid custom of making fun of the teachers, to standing treat by turns at the school teashop, to jungle games in which we went galloping about the school woods, and to dormitory life. I took part in all these diversions except dormitory life. My ever-cautious parents had used the plea of my poor health to obtain for me an exception to the rule requiring every student to live in the dormitory for a year or two during his middle-school course. And once again their main reason was nothing more than to keep me from learning "bad things."

The number of day students was small. In the final term of our second year a newcomer joined our little group. This was Omi. He had been expelled from the dormitory because of some outrageous behavior. Until then I had paid no particular attention to him, but when his expulsion placed this unmistakable brand of what is called "delinquency" upon him, I suddenly found it difficult to keep my eyes off him.

One day a good-natured, fat friend came running up to me, giggling and showing his dimples. By these familiar signs I knew he had come into possession of some secret information.

"But do I have something to tell you!" he said.

I left the side of the radiator and went out into the corridor with my good-natured friend. We leaned on a window overlooking the wind-swept archery court. That window was our usual spot for telling secrets.

"Well, Omi—" my friend began. Then he stopped, blushing as though he was too embarrassed to continue. (Once, in about the fifth year of lower school, when we had all been talking about "that," this boy had flatly contradicted us with a capital remark: "It's all a complete lie—I absolutely know people do no such thing." Another time, upon hearing that a friend's father had palsy, he warned me that palsy was contageous and that I had better not get too near that friend.)

"Hey! what gives with Omi?" Though I was still using the polite, feminine forms of speech at home, when at school I had begun speaking crudely like the other boys.

"This is the truth. That guy Omi—well, they say he's already had lots of girls, that's what!"

It was easy to believe. Omi must have been several years older than the rest of us, having failed to be promoted two or three times. He surpassed us all in physique, and in the contours of his face could be seen signs of some privileged youthfulness excelling ours by far. He had an innate and lofty manner of gratuitous scorn. There was not one single thing that he found undeserving of contempt. For us there was no changing the fact that an honor student was an honor student, a teacher a teacher; that policemen or university students or office workers were precisely policemen, university students, and office workers. In the same way Omi was simply Omi, and it was impossible to escape his contemptuous eyes and scornful laughter.

"Really?" I said. And for some unknown reason I thought instantly of Omi's deft hands cleaning the rifles we used for military training. I remembered his smart appearance as a squad leader, the special favorite only of the drillmaster and the gymnastics instructor.

"That's why—that's the reason why—" My friend

gave the lewd snicker that only middle-school boys can understand. "Well, they say his you-know-what is awful big. Next time there's a game of Dirty just you feel and see. That'll prove it."

"Dirty" was a traditional sport at our school, always widespread among the boys during their first and second years, and as is the case with any craze for a pastime, it was more like a morbid disease than an amusement. We played it in broad daylight, in full public view. Some boy—call him A—would be standing around not keeping his wits about him. Noticing this, another boy—B—would dart up from the side and make a well-aimed grab. If his grab was successful, B would then retreat victoriously to a distance and begin hooting:

"Oh, it's big! Oh, what a big one A has!"

Whatever the impetus behind the game may have been, its sole objective seemed to be the sight of the comical figure cut by the victim as he dropped his schoolbooks, or anything else he might be carrying, and used both hands to protect the spot under attack. Actually, the boys discovered in the sport their own shame, brought into the open by their laughter; and then, from a secure foothold of still louder laughter, they had the satisfaction of ridiculing their common shame, as personified in this victim's blushing cheeks.

As though by prearrangement, the victim would shout:

"Oh, that B—he's dirty!"

Then the bystanders would chime in with a chorus of assent:

"Oh, that B—he's dirty!"

Omi was in his element in this game. His attacks almost always ended swiftly in success, so much so as to give cause for wondering if the boys did not secretly look forward to being attacked by Omi. And, in return, his victims were constantly seeking revenge. But none of their attempts on him were ever successful. He always walked around with one hand in his pocket, and the moment he was ambushed he would instantly fashion twofold armor out of the hand in his pocket and his free hand.

Those words of my friend were like fertilizer poured over the poisonous weed of an idea deeply planted in me. Until then I had joined in the games of Dirty with feelings as completely naïve as those of the other boys. But my friend's words seemed to bring my "bad habit" —that solitary life which I had been unconsciously keeping strictly segregated—into an inseparable relationship with this game, with this my communal life. That such a connection had been established in my mind was made certain by the fact that suddenly, whether I would or no, his words "feel and see" had become charged with a special significance for me, a significance that none of my innocent friends would ever have understood.

From that time on I no longer participated in games of Dirty. I was fearful of the moment when I might have to attack Omi, and even more of the moment when Omi might attack me. I was always on the lookout, and when there were indications that the game might break out—like a riot or rebellion, it could arise from the most casual event—I would get out of the way and keep my eyes glued on Omi from a safe distance. . . .

As a matter of fact, Omi's influence had already begun to seduce us even before we were aware of it. For example, there were the socks. By those days the corrosion of an educational system that aimed at producing soldiers had already reached even our school; General Enoki's deathbed precept—"Be Simple and Manly" —had been reheated and served up; and such things as gaudy mufflers or socks were taboo. In fact, any muffler at all was frowned upon, and the rule was that shirts be white and socks black, or at least of a solid color. It was Omi alone who never failed to wear a white-silk muffler and bold-patterned socks.

This first defier of the taboo possessed an uncanny skill for clothing his wickedness in the fair name of revolt. Through his own experience he had discovered what a weakness boys have for the charms of revolt. In front of the drillmaster—this country bumpkin of a non-commissioned officer was a bosom friend of Omi's or, rather, it seemed, his henchman—he would deliberately take his time in wrapping his muffler about his neck and ostentatiously turning back the lapels of his gold-buttoned overcoat in the Napoleonic manner.

As is ever the case, however, the revolt of the blind masses did not go beyond a niggardly imitation. Hoping to escape the dangers entailed and taste only the joys of revolt, we pirated nothing from Omi's daring example except his socks. And, in this instance, I too was one of the crowd.

Arriving at school in the morning, we would chatter boisterously in the classroom before lessons began, not sitting in the seats, but on the tops of the desks. Anyone who came wearing gaudy socks with a novel pattern would make a great show of plucking up the creases of his trousers as he sat down on a desk. At once he would be rewarded with keen-eyed cries of admiration:

"Oh! flashy socks!"

Our vocabulary did not contain any tribute of praise surpassing the word flashy. Omi never put in an appearance until the last moment, just before class formation; but the instant we said flashy, a mental picture of his haughty glance would rise before us all, speaker and hearer alike.

One morning just after a snowfall I went to school very early. The evening before, a friend had telephoned saying there was going to be a snowfight the next morning. Being by nature given to wakefulness the night before any greatly anticipated event, I had no sooner opened my eyes too early the next morning than I set out for school, heedless of the time.

The snow scarcely reached my shoetops. And later, as I looked down at the city from a window of the elevated train, the snow scene, not yet having caught the rays of the rising sun, looked more gloomy than beautiful. The snow seemed like a dirty bandage hiding the open wounds of the city, hiding those irregular gashes of haphazard streets and tortuous alleys, courtyards and occasional plots of bare ground, that form the only beauty to be found in the panorama of our cities.

When the train, still almost empty, was nearing the station for my school, I saw the sun rise beyond the factory district. The scene suddenly became one of joy and light. Now the columns of ominously towering smokestacks and the somber rise and fall of the monotonous slate-colored roofs cowered behind the noisy laughter of the brightly shining snow mask. It is just such a snow-covered landscape that often becomes the tragic setting for riot or revolution. And even the faces of the passers-by, suspiciously wan in the reflection of the snow, reminded me somehow of conspirators.

When I got off at the station in front of the school, the snow was already melting, and I could hear the water running off the roof of the forwarding company next door. I could not shake the illusion that it was the radiance which was splashing down. Bright and shining slivers of it were suicidally hurling themselves at the sham quagmire of the pavement, all smeared with the slush of passing shoes. As I walked under the eaves, one sliver hurled itself by mistake at the nape of my neck. . . .

Inside the school gates there was not yet a single footprint in the snow. The locker room was still closed fast, but the other rooms were open.

I opened a window of the second-year classroom, which was on the ground floor, and looked out at the snow in the grove behind the school. There in the path that came from the rear gate, up the slope of the grove, and led to the building I was in, I could see large footprints; they came up along the path and continued to a spot directly below the window from which I was looking. Then the footprints turned back and disappeared behind the science building, which could be seen on a diagonal to the left.

Someone had already come. It was plain that he had ascended the path from the rear gate, looked into the classroom through the window, and seeing that no one was there, walked on by himself to the rear of the science building. Only a few of the day students came to school by way of the rear gate. It was rumored that Omi, who was one of those few, came each morning from some woman's house. But he would never put in an appearance until the last moment before class formation. Nevertheless, I could not imagine who else might have made the footprints, and judging by their large size, I was convinced they were his.

Leaning out the window and straining my eyes, I saw the color of fresh black soil in the shoe tracks, making them seem somehow determined and powerful. An indescribable force drew me toward those shoe prints. I felt that I should like to throw myself head-first out of the window to bury my face in them. But, as usual, my sluggish motor nerves protected me from my sudden whim. Instead of diving out the window, I put my satchel on a desk and then scrambled slowly up onto the window sill. The hooks and eyes on the front of my uniform jacket had scarcely pressed against the stone window sill before they were at daggers' point with my frail ribs, producing a pain mixed with a sort of sorrowful sweetness. After I had jumped from the window onto the snow, the slight pain remained as a pleasant stimulus, filling me with a trembling emotion of adventure. I fitted my overshoes carefully into the footprints.

The prints had looked quite large, but now I found they were almost the same size as mine. I had failed to take into account the fact that the person who had made them was probably wearing overshoes too, as was the vogue among us in those days. Now that the thought occurred to me, I decided the footprints were not large enough to be Omi's.

And yet, despite my uneasy feeling that I would be

disappointed in my immediate hope of finding Omi behind the science building, I was still somehow compelled by the idea of following after the black shoe-prints. Probably at this point I was no longer motivated solely by the hope of finding Omi, but instead, at the sight of the violated mystery, was seized with a mixed feeling of yearning and revenge toward the person who had come before me and left his footprints in the snow.

Breathing hard, I began following the tracks.

As though walking on steppingstones, I went moving my feet from footprint to footprint. The outlines of the prints revealed now glassy, coal-black earth, now dead turf, now soiled, packed snow, now paving stones. Suddenly I discovered that, without being aware of it, I had fallen into walking with long strides, exactly like Omi's.

Following the tracks to the rear of the science building, I passed through the long shadow the building threw over the snow, and then continued on to the high ground overlooking the wide athletic field. Because of the mantle of glittering snow that covered everything, the three-hundred-meter ellipse of the track could not be distinguished from the undulating field it enclosed. In a corner of the field two great zelkova trees stood close together, and their shadows, greatly elongated in the morning sun, fell across the snow, lending meaning to the scene, providing the happy imperfection with which Nature always accents grandeur. The great elm-like trees towered up with a plastic delicacy in the blue winter sky, in the reflection of the snow from below, in the lateral rays of the morning sun; and occasionally some snow slipped down like gold dust from the crotches formed against the tree trunks by the stark, leafless branches. The roof ridges of the boys' dormitories, standing in a row beyond the athletic field, and the copse beyond them seemed to be motionless in sleep. Everything was so silent that even the soundless slipping of the snow seemed to echo loud and wide.

For a moment I could not see a thing in this expanse of glare.

The snow scene was in a way like a fresh castle ruin: this legerdemain was being bathed in that same boundless light and splendor which exists solely in the ruins of ancient castles. And there in one corner of the ruin, in the snow of the almost five-meter-wide track, enormous Roman letters had been drawn. Nearest to me was a large circle, an *O*. Next came an *M*. And beyond it a third letter was still in the process of being written, a tall and thick *I*.

It was Omi. The footprints I had followed led to the *O*, from the *O* to the *M*, and arrived finally at the figure of Omi himself, just then dragging his overshoes over the snow to finish his *I*, looking downward from above his white muffler, both hands thrust in his overcoat pockets. His shadow stretched defiantly across the snow, running parallel with the shadows of the zelkova trees in the field.

My cheeks were on fire. I made a snowball in my gloved hands and threw it at him. It fell short.

Just then he finished writing the *I* and, probably by chance, looked in my direction.

"Hey!" I shouted.

Although I feared that Omi's only reaction would be one of displeasure, I was impelled by an indescribable passion, and no sooner had I shouted out than I found myself running down the steep slope toward him. As I ran, a most undreamed-of sound came reverberating toward me—a friendly shout from him, filled with his power:

"Hey, don't step on the letters!"

He certainly seemed to be a different person this morning. As a rule, even when he went home he never did his homework, but left his schoolbooks in his locker and came to school in the mornings with both hands thrust in his overcoat pockets, barely in time to shed his coat dexterously and fall in at the tail end of class formation. What a change today! Not only must he have been whiling away the time by himself since early morning, but now he welcomed me with his inimitable smile, both friendly and rough at the same time—welcomed me, whom he had always treated as a snot-nosed child, beneath contempt. How I had been longing for that smile, the flash of those youthful white teeth!

But when I got close enough to see his smiling face distinctly, my heart lost its passion of the moment before, when I had shouted "Hey!" Now, suddenly, I became paralyzed with timidity. I was pulled up short by the flashing realization that at heart Omi was a lonely person. His smile was probably assumed in order to hide the weak spot in his armor, which my understanding had chanced upon, but this fact did not hurt me so much as it hurt the image I had been constructing of him.

The instant I had seen that enormous OMI drawn in the snow, I had understood, perhaps half-unconsciously, all the nooks and corners of his loneliness—understood also the real motive, probably not clearly understood even by himself, that brought him to school this early in the morning. . . . If my idol had now mentally bent his knee to me, offering some such excuse as "I came early for the snow fight," I would certainly have lost from within me something even more important than the pride he would have lost. Feeling it was up to me to speak, I nervously tried to think of something to say.

"The snowfight's out for today, isn't it?" I finally said. "I thought it was going to snow more though."

"H'm." He assumed an expression of indifference. The strong outline of his jaw hardened again in his cheeks, and a sort of pitying disdain toward me revived. He was obviously making an effort to regard me as a child, and his eyes again began to gleam insolently. In one part of his mind he must have been grateful to me for not making a single inquiry about his letters in the snow, and I was fascinated by the painful efforts he was making to overcome this feeling of gratitude.

"Humph! I hate wearing children's gloves," he said.

"But even grownups wear wool gloves like these."

"Poor thing, I bet you don't even know how leather gloves feel. Here—"

Abruptly he thrust his snow-drenched leather gloves against my cheeks.

I dodged. A raw carnal feeling blazed up within me, branding my cheeks. I felt myself staring at him with crystal-clear eyes. . . .

From that time on I was in love with Omi.

For me this was the first love in my life. And, if such a blunt way of speaking be forgiven, it was clearly a love closely connected with desires of the flesh.

I began looking forward impatiently to summer, or at least to summer's beginning. Surely, I thought, summer will bring with it an opportunity to see his naked body. Also, I cherished deeply within me a still more shamefaced desire. This was to see that "big thing" of his.

On the switchboard of my memory two pairs of gloves have crossed wires—those leather gloves of Omi's and a pair of white ceremonial gloves. I never seem to be able to decide which memory might be real, which false. Perhaps the leather gloves were more in harmony with his coarse features. And yet again, precisely because of his coarse features, perhaps it was the white pair which became him more.

Coarse features—even though I use the words, actually such a description is nothing more than that of the impression created by the ordinary face of one lone young man mixed in among boys. Unrivaled though his build was, in height he was by no means the tallest among us. The pretentious uniform our school required, resembling a naval officer's, could scarcely hang well on our still-immature bodies, and Omi alone filled his with a sensation of solid weight and a sort of sexuality. Surely I was not the only one who looked with envious and loving eyes at the muscles of his shoulders and chest, that sort of muscle which can be spied out even beneath a blue-serge uniform.

Something like a secret feeling of superiority was always hovering about his face. Perhaps it was that sort of feeling which blazes higher and higher the more one's pride is hurt. It seemed that, for Omi, such misfortunes as failures in examinations and expulsions were the symbols of a frustrated will. The will to what? I imagined vaguely that it must be some purpose toward which his "evil genius" was driving him. And I was certain that even he did not yet know the full purport of this vast conspiracy against him.

Something about his face gave one the sensation of

abundant blood coursing richly throughout his body; it was a round face, with haughty cheekbones rising from swarthy cheeks, lips that seemed to have been sewn into a fine line, sturdy jaws, and a broad but well-shaped and not too prominent nose. These features were the clothing for an untamed soul. How could anyone have expected such a person to have a secret, inner life? All one could hope to find in him was the pattern of that forgotten perfection which the rest of us have lost in some far distant past.

There were times when a whim would bring him peering into the books, erudite and far beyond my years, that I was reading. I would almost always give him a noncommittal smile and close whatever book I was holding, to keep him from seeing it. It was not out of shame: rather, I was pained by any indication that he might have an interest in such things as books, might reveal an awkwardness about them, might seem to weary of his own unconscious perfection. I found it bitter to think that this fisherman might forget, desert, deny the Ionia of his birth.

I watched Omi incessantly, both in the classroom and on the playgrounds. While doing so, I fashioned a perfect, flawless illusion of him. Hence it is that I cannot discover a single flaw in the image that remains imprinted on my memory. In a piece of writing such as this, a character should be brought to life by describing some essential idiosyncrasy, some lovable fault, but from my memory of Omi I can extract not a single such imperfection. There were, however, numberless other impressions that I got from Omi, of infinite variety, all filled with delicate nuances. In a phrase, what I did derive from him was a precise definition of the perfection of life and manhood, personified in his eyebrows, his forehead, his eyes, his nose, his ears, his cheeks, his cheekbones, his lips, his jaws, the nape of his neck, his throat, his complexion, the color of his skin, his strength, his chest, his hands, and countless other of his attributes.

With these as a basis, the principle of selection came into operation, and I completed a systematic structure of likes and dislikes: Because of him I cannot love an intellectual person. Because of him I am not attracted to a person who wears glasses. Because of him I began to love strength, an impression of overflowing blood, ignorance, rough gestures, careless speech, and the savage melancholy inherent in flesh not tainted in any way with intellect. . . .

And yet, from the outset, a logical impossibility was involved for me in these rude tastes, making my desires forever unattainable. As a rule there is nothing more logical than the carnal impulse. But in my case, no sooner would I begin to share intellectual understanding with a person who had attracted me than my desire for that person would collapse. The discovery of even the slightest intellectualism in a companion would force me to a rational judgment of values. In a reciprocal relationship such as love, one must give the same thing he demands from the other; hence my desire for ignorance in a companion required, however temporarily, an unconditional "revolt against reason" on my part. But for me such a revolt was absolutely impossible.

Thus, when confronting those possessors of sheer animal flesh unspoiled by intellect—young toughs, sailors, soldiers, fishermen—there was nothing for me to do but be forever watching them from afar with impassioned indifference, being careful never to exchange words with them. Probably the only place in which I could have lived at ease would have been some uncivilized tropical land where I could not speak the language. Now that I think of it, I realize that from earliest childhood I felt a yearning toward those intense summers of the kind that are seething forever in savage lands. . . .

Well, then, there were the white gloves of which I was going to speak.

At my school it was the custom to wear white gloves on ceremonial days. Just to pull on a pair of white gloves, with mother-of-pearl buttons shining gloomily at the wrists and three meditative rows of stitching on the backs, was enough to evoke the symbols of all ceremonial days—the somber assembly hall where the ceremonies were held, the box of Shioze sweets received upon leaving, the cloudless skies under which such days always seem to make brilliant sounds in midcourse and then collapse.

It was on a national holiday in winter, undoubtedly Empire Day. That morning again Omi had come to school unusually early.

The second-year students had already driven the freshmen away from the swinging-log on the playground at the side of the school buildings, taking cruel delight in doing so, and were now in full possession. Although outwardly scornful of such childish playground equipment as the swinging-log, the second-year students still had a lingering affection for it in their hearts, and by forcibly driving the freshmen away, they were able to adopt the face-saving pretense of indulging in the amusement half-derisively, without any seriousness. The freshmen had formed a circle at a distance around the log and were watching the rough play of the upperclassmen, who, in turn, were quite conscious of having an audience. The log, suspended on chains, swung back and forth rhythmically, with a battering-ram motion, and the contest was to make each other fall off the log.

Omi was standing with both feet planted firmly at the mid-point of the log, eagerly looking around for opponents; it was a posture that made him look exactly like a murderer brought to bay.

No one in our class was a match for him. Already several boys had jumped up onto the log, one after another, only to be cut down by Omi's quick hands; their feet had trampled away the frost on the earth around the log, which had been glittering in the early morning sunlight.

After each victory Omi would clasp his hands to-gether over his head like a triumphant boxer, smiling profusely. And the first-year students would cheer, al-ready forgetting he had been a ringleader in driving them away from the log.

My eyes followed his white-gloved hands. They were moving fiercely, but with marvelous precision, like the paws of some young beast, a wolf perhaps. From time to time they would cut through the winter-morning's air, like the feathers of an arrow, straight to the chest of an opponent. And always the opponent would fall to the frosty ground, landing now on his feet, now on his buttocks. On rare occasions, at the moment of knocking an opponent off the log, Omi himself would be on the verge of falling; as he fought to regain the equilibrium of his careening body, he would appear to be writhing in agony there atop the log, made slippery by the faintly gleaming frost. But always the strength in his supple hips would restore him once again to that assassin-like posture.

The log was moving left and right impersonally, swinging in unperturbed arcs. . . .

As I watched, I was suddenly overcome with uneasi-ness, with a racking, inexplicable uneasiness. It re-sembled a dizziness such as might have come from watching the swaying of the log, but it was not that. Probably it was more a mental vertigo, an uneasiness in which my inner equilibrium was on the point of being destroyed by the sight of his every perilous movement.

And this instability was made even more precarious by the fact that within it two contrary forces were pulling at me, contending for supremacy. One was the instinct of self-preservation. The second force—which was bent, even more profoundly, more intensely, upon the complete disintegration of my inner balance—was a compulsion toward suicide, that subtle and secret impulse to which a person often unconsciously surrenders himself.

"What's the matter with you, you bunch of cowards! Isn't there anyone else?"

Omi's body was gently swinging to the right and left, his hips bending with the motions of the log. He placed his white-gloved hands on his hips. The gilded badge on his cap glittered in the morning sun. I had never seen him so handsome as at that moment.

"I'll do it!" I cried.

My heartbeats had steadily increased in violence, and using them as a measure, I had exactly estimated the moment when I would finally say these words. It has always been thus with moments in which I yield to desire. It seemed to me that my going and standing against Omi on that log was a predestined fact, rather than merely an impulsive action. In later years, such actions as this misled me into thinking I was "a man of strong will."

"Watch out! Watch out! You'll get licked," everyone shouted.

Amid their cheers of derision I climbed up on one end of the log. While I was trying to get up, my feet began slipping, and again the air was full of noisy jeers.

Omi greeted me with a clowning face. He played the fool with all his might and pretended to be slipping. Again, he would tease me by fluttering his gloved fingers at me. To my eyes those fingers were the sharp points of some dangerous weapon, about to run me through.

The palms of our white-gloved hands met many times in stinging slaps, and each time I reeled under the force of the blow. It was obvious that he was deliberately holding back his strength, as though wanting to make sport of me to his heart's content, postponing what would otherwise have been my quick defeat.

"Oh! I'm frightened—How strong you are!—I'm licked. I'm just about to fall—look at me!" He stuck out his tongue and pretended to fall.

It was unbearably painful for me to see his clownish face, to see him unwittingly destroy his own beauty. Even though I was now gradually being forced back along the log, I could not keep from lowering my eyes. And just at that instant I was caught by a swoop of his right hand. In a reflex action to keep from falling, I clutched at the air with my right hand and, by some chance, managed to fasten onto the fingertips of his right hand. I grasped a vivid sensation of his fingers fitting closely inside the white gloves.

For an instant he and I looked each other in the eye.

It was truly only an instant. The clownish look had vanished, and, instead, his face was suffused with a strangely candid expression. An immaculate, fierce something, neither hostility nor hatred, was vibrating there like a bowstring. Or perhaps this was only my imagination. Perhaps it was nothing but the stark, empty look of the instant in which, pulled by the fingertips, he felt himself losing his balance. However that may have been, I knew intuitively and certainly that Omi had seen the way I looked at him in that instant, had felt the pulsating force that flowed like lightning between our fingertips, and had guessed my secret— that I was in love with him, with no one in the world but him.

At almost the same moment the two of us fell tumbling off the log.

I was helped to my feet. It was Omi who helped me. He pulled me up roughly by the arm and, saying not a word, brushed the dirt off my uniform. His elbows and gloves were stained with a mixture of dirt and glittering frost.

He took my arm and began walking away with me. I looked up into his face as though reproving him for this show of intimacy.

At my school we had all been classmates since lower-school days, and there was nothing unusual about putting arms about each other's shoulders. As a matter of fact, at that moment the whistle for class formation sounded and everyone hurried off in just that intimate way. The fact that Omi had tumbled to the ground with me was for them nothing but the conclusion of a game they had already gradually become bored with watching, and even the fact that Omi and I walked away together with linked arms could hardly have been a sight worthy of particular notice.

For all that, it was a supreme delight I felt as I walked leaning on his arm. Perhaps because of my frail constitution, I usually felt a premonition of evil mixed in with every joy; but on this occasion I felt nothing but the fierce, intense sensation of his arm: it seemed to be transmitted from his arm to mine and, once having gained entry, to spread out until it flooded my entire body. I felt that I should like to walk thus with him to the end of the earth.

But we arrived at the place for class formation, where, too soon, he let go of my arm and took his place in line. Thereafter he did not look around in my direction. During the ceremony that followed, he sat four seats away from me. Time and time again I looked from the stains on my own white gloves to those on Omi's. . . .

My blind adoration of Omi was devoid of any element of conscious criticism, and still less did I have anything like a moral viewpoint where he was concerned. Whenever I tried to capture the amorphous mass of my adoration within the confines of analysis, it would already have disappeared. If there be such a thing as love that has neither duration nor progress, this was precisely my emotion. The eyes through which I saw Omi were always those of a "first glance" or, if I may say so, of the "primeval glance." It was purely an unconscious attitude on my part, a ceaseless effort to protect my fourteen-year-old purity from the process of erosion.

Could this have been love? Grant it to be one form of love, for even though at first glance it seemed to retain its pristine form forever, simply repeating that form over and over again, it too had its own unique sort of debasement and decay. And it was a debasement more evil than that of any normal kind of love. Indeed, of all the kinds of decay in this world, decadent purity is the most malignant.

Nevertheless, in my unrequited love for Omi, in this the first love I encountered in life, I seemed like a baby bird keeping its truly innocent animal lusts hidden under its wing. I was being tempted, not by the desire for possession, but simply by unadorned temptation itself.

To say the least, while at school, particularly during a boring class, I could not take my eyes off Omi's profile. What more could I have done when I did not know that to love is both to seek and to be sought? For me love was nothing but a dialogue of little riddles, with no answers given. As for my spirit of adoration, I never even imagined it to be a thing that required some sort of answer.

One day I had a cold and, even though it was not at all serious, stayed home from school. Upon returning to school the next day, I discovered that the day I had chosen to miss had been nothing less than the day of the first spring physical examination in our third year. Several other students had likewise missed the examination, and we all went along together to the medical office.

In the office a gas stove was sending up such a feeble blue flame into the sunlight that one could not even be certain it was lit. There was nothing but the smell of disinfectants. Nowhere was there that pale-pink smell, like hot sugared milk, so characteristic of a room where a crowd of boys are awaiting a physical examination, their naked bodies pushing and jostling against each other. Instead there was only a handful of us, taking off our clothes in silence, shivering miserably. . . .

There was a skinny boy who, like me, was always catching cold. He was standing on the scales, and as I looked at his pale, bony back, covered with down, I suddenly remembered my everlasting, fierce desire to see Omi's naked body. I realized how stupid I had been not to have foreseen what a perfect opportunity the physical examination of the day before would have provided for achieving that desire. Now the opportunity was already lost; there was nothing to do but go on awaiting some random chance in the future.

I turned pale. In the pallid goose-flesh that suddenly covered me I was experiencing a form of regret like some piercing cold. I stared vacantly into the air, scratching the ugly vaccination scars on my thin arms. My name was called. The scales looked exactly like a scaffold proclaiming the hour of my execution.

"Eighty-eight," the assistant barked to the school doctor. This assistant had formerly been an orderly in a military hospital and still retained the bearing.

As the doctor entered the figure on my card, he was mumbling to himself:

"Wish he'd get to ninety pounds at least."

I had become used to undergoing this treatment at every physical examination. But today I was so relieved that Omi was not present to witness my humiliation that the doctor's words did not cause me the usual anguish. For an instant my feeling of relief amounted almost to joy. . . .

"All right—next!"

The assistant shoved my shoulder impatiently. But this time I did not glare back at him with the hateful and irritable look I usually gave him.

Nevertheless, even though dimly, I must have foreseen the ending of my first love. In all likelihood it was the uneasiness created by this foreboding that formed the nucleus of my pleasure.

There came a day in late spring that was like a tailor's sample cut from a bolt of summer, or like a dress rehearsal for the coming season. It was that day of the year that comes as Summer's representative, to inspect everyone's clothing chest and make sure all is in readiness. It was that day on which people appear in summer shirts to show they have passed muster.

Despite the warmth of the day, I had a cold, and my bronchial tubes were irritated. One of my friends happened to be suffering with an upset stomach, and we went together to the medical office to get written excuses that would permit us merely to watch gymnastic exercises without having to participate.

On our way back, we walked along toward the gymnasium as slowly as possible. Our visit to the medical office provided us with a good reason for being tardy, and we were anxious to shorten even by a little the boring time we would have to spend watching the gymnastics.

"My, it's hot, isn't it?" I said, taking off the jacket of my uniform.

"You'd better not do that, not with a cold. And they'll make you do gymnastics anyway if they see you that way."

I put my jacket on again hurriedly.

"But it'll be all right for me, because it's only my stomach." And, instead of me, it was my friend who ostentatiously took off his jacket, as though taunting me.

Arriving at the gymnasium, we saw by the clothing

hanging on the hooks along the wall that all the boys had taken off their sweaters, and some even their shirts. The area round the outdoor exercise bars, where there was sand and grass, seemed to be blazing brightly as we looked out at it from the dark gymnasium. My sickly constitution produced its usual reaction, and I walked toward the exercise bars giving my petulant little coughs.

The insignificant gymnastics instructor scarcely glanced at the medical excuses which we handed him. Instead he turned immediately to the waiting boys and said:

"All right now, let's try the horizontal bar. Omi, you show them how it's done."

Friendly voices began calling Omi's name stealthily. He had simply evaporated, as he often did during gymnastics. There was no knowing what he did on these occasions, but this time again he came lounging out from behind a tree whose young green leaves were trembling with light.

When I saw him my heart set up a clamor in my breast. He had taken off his shirt, leaving nothing but a dazzlingly white, sleeveless undershirt to cover his chest. His swarthy skin made the pure whiteness of the undershirt look almost too clean. It was a whiteness that could almost be smelled from a distance, like plaster of Paris. And that white plaster was carved in relief, showing the bold contours of his chest and its two nipples.

"The horizontal bar is it?" he asked the instructor, speaking curtly, with a tone of confidence.

"Yes, that's right."

Then, with that haughty indolence so often exhibited by the possessors of fine physiques, Omi stretched his hands down leisurely to the ground and smeared his palms with damp sand from just beneath the surface. Rising, he brushed his hands together roughly, and turned his face upward toward the iron bar. His eyes flashed with the bold resolve of one who defies the gods, and for a moment their pupils mirrored the clouds and blue skies of May, along with a cold disdain.

A leap shot through him. Instantly his body was hanging from the iron bar, suspended there by those two strong arms of his, arms certainly worthy of being tattooed with anchors.

"Ahhh!" The admiring exclamation of his classmates arose and floated thickly in the air.

Any one of the boys could have looked into his heart and discovered that his admiration was not aroused simply by Omi's feat of strength. It was admiration for youth, for life, for supremacy. And it was astonishment at the abundant growth of hair that Omi's upraised arms had revealed in his armpits.

This was probably the first time we had seen such an opulence of hair; it seemed almost prodigal, like some luxuriant growth of troublesome summer weeds. And in the same way that such weeds, not satisfied to have completely covered a summer garden, will even spread up a stone staircase, the hair overflowed the deeply carved banks of Omi's armpits and spread thickly toward his chest. Those two black thickets gleamed glossily, bathed in sunlight, and the surprising whiteness of his skin there was like white sand peeping through.

As he began the pull-up, the muscles of his arms bulged out hard, and his shoulders swelled like summer clouds. The thickets of his armpits were folded into dark shadows, gradually becoming invisible. And at last his chest rubbed high against the iron bar, trembling there delicately. With a repetition of these same motions, he did a rapid series of pull-ups.

Life-force—it was the sheer extravagant abundance of life-force that overpowered the boys. They were overwhelmed by the feeling he gave of having too much life, by the feeling of purposeless violence that can be explained only as life existing for its own sake, by his type of ill-humored, unconcerned exuberance. Without his being aware of it, some force had stolen into Omi's flesh and was scheming to take possession of him, to crash through him, to spill out of him, to outshine him. In this respect the power resembled a malady. Infected with this violent power, his flesh had been put on this earth for no other reason than to become an insane human-sacrifice, one without any fear of infection. Persons who live in terror of infection cannot but regard such flesh as a bitter reproach. . . . The boys staggered back, away from him.

As for me, I felt the same as the other boys—with important differences. In my case—it was enough to make me blush with shame—I had had an erection, from the first moment in which I had glimpsed that abundance of his. I was wearing light-weight spring trousers and was afraid the other boys might notice what had happened to me. And, even leaving aside this fear, there was yet another emotion in my heart, which was certainly not unalloyed rapture. Here I was, looking upon the naked body I had so longed to see, and the shock of seeing it had unexpectedly unleashed an emotion within me that was the opposite of joy.

It was jealousy. . . .

Omi dropped to the ground with the air of a person who had accomplished some noble deed. Hearing the thud of his fall, I closed my eyes and shook my head. Then I told myself that I was no longer in love with Omi.

It was jealousy. It was jealousy fierce enough to make me voluntarily forswear my love of Omi.

Probably the need I began to feel about this time for a Spartan course in self-discipline was involved in this situation. (The fact that I am writing this book is already one example of my continued efforts in that direction.) Due to my sickliness and the doting care which I had received ever since I was a baby, I had always been too timid even to look people directly in the eye. But now I became obsessed with a single motto —"Be Strong!"

To that end I hit upon an exercise that consisted of scowling fixedly into the face of this or that passenger on the streetcars in which I went back and forth to school. Most of the passengers, whom I chose indiscriminately, showed no particular signs of fear upon being scowled at by a pale, weak boy, but simply looked the other way as though annoyed; only rarely would one of them scowl back. When they looked away I counted it a triumph. In this way I gradually trained myself to look people in the eye. . . .

Having once decided that I had renounced love, I dismissed all further thought of it from my mind. This was a hasty conclusion, lacking in perception. I was failing to take into acount one of the clearest evidences there is of sexual love—the phenomenon of erection. Over a truly long period of time I had my erections, and also indulged in that "bad habit" which incited them whenever I was alone, without ever becoming aware of the significance of my actions. Although already in possession of the usual information concerning sex, I was not yet troubled with the sense of being different.

I do not mean to say that I viewed those desires of mine that deviated from accepted standards as normal and orthodox; nor do I mean that I labored under the mistaken impression that my friends possessed the same desires. Surprisingly enough, I was so engrossed in tales of romance that I devoted all my elegant dreams to thoughts of love between man and maid, and to marriage, exactly as though I were a young girl who knew nothing of the world. I tossed my love for Omi onto the rubbish heap of neglected riddles, never once searching deeply for its meaning. Now when I write the word love, when I write affection, my meaning is totally different from my understanding of the words at that time. I never even dreamed that such desires as I had felt toward Omi might have a significant connection with the realities of my "life."

And yet some instinct within me demanded that I seek solitude, that I remain apart as something different. This compulsion was manifested as a mysterious and strange malaise. I have already described how during my childhood I was weighed down by a sense of uneasiness at the thought of becoming an adult, and my feeling of growing up continued to be accompanied by a strange, piercing unrest.

During my growing years a deep tuck was sewn into every pair of new trousers so that they could be lengthened each year, and just as in any other family, my steadily increasing height was recorded by successive pencil marks on one of the pillars of the house. The little ceremony of these periodic measurings always took place in the sitting room under the eyes of all the family, and each time they teased me and found a simple-minded pleasure in the fact that I had grown taller. I would respond with forced smiles.

Actually, the thought that I might reach the height of an adult filled me with a foreboding of some fearful danger. On the one hand, my indefinable feeling of unrest increased my capacity for dreams divorced from all reality and, on the other, drove me toward the "bad habit" that caused me to take refuge in those dreams. The restlessness was my excuse. . . .

"You'll surely die before you're twenty," a friend once said to me jokingly, referring to my weak constitution.

"What an awful thing to say!" I replied, screwing my face up into a bitter smile. But actually his prediction had a strangely sweet and romantic attraction for me.

"Want to make a bet on it?" he went on.

"But if you bet I'll die, there'd be nothing for me to do but bet I'll live."

"That's right, isn't it? It's a shame, isn't it?" my friend said, speaking with all the ruthlessness of youth. "You'd certainly lose, wouldn't you?"

It was true—not only of me, but of all the students my age—that nothing approaching Omi's maturity could yet be discerned in our armpits. Instead there was only the faintest promise of buds that might yet burgeon. For this reason I had never before paid any particular attention to that part of my body. It was undoubtedly the sight of the hair under Omi's arms that day which made the armpit a fetish for me.

It got so that whenever I took a bath I would stand before the mirror a long time, staring at the mirror's ungracious reflection of my naked body. It was another case of the ugly duckling who believed he would become a swan, except that this time that heroic fairy tale was to have an exactly reverse outcome. Even though my scrawny shoulders and narrow chest had not the slightest resemblance to Omi's, I looked at them closely in the mirror and forcibly found reasons for believing I would someday have a chest like Omi's, shoulders like Omi's. But in spite of this, a thin ice of uneasiness formed here and there over the surface of my heart. It was more than uneasiness: it was a sort of masochistic conviction, a conviction as firm as though founded on divine revelation, a conviction that made me tell myself: "Never in this world can you resemble Omi."

In the woodblock prints of the Genroku period one often finds the features of a pair of lovers to be surprisingly similar, with little to distinguish the man from the woman. The universal ideal of beauty in Greek sculpture likewise approaches a close resemblance between the male and female. Might this not be one of the secrets of love? Might it not be that through the innermost recesses of love there courses an unattainable longing in which both the man and the woman desire to become the exact image of the other? Might not this longing drive them on, leading at last to a tragic reaction in which they seek to attain the impossible by going to the opposite extreme? In short, since their mutual love cannot achieve a perfection of mutual identity, is there not a mental process whereby each of them tries instead to emphasize their points of dissimilarity—the man his manliness and the woman her womanliness—and uses this very revolt as a form of coquetry toward the other? Or if they do achieve a similarity, it unfortunately lasts for only a fleeting moment of illusion. Because, as the girl becomes more bold and the boy more shy, there comes an instant at which they pass each other going in opposite directions, overshooting their mark and passing on beyond to some point where the mark no longer exists.

Viewed in this light, my jealousy—jealousy fierce enough to make me tell myself I had renounced my love—was all the more love. I had ended by loving those "things like Omi's" that, by slow degrees, diffidently, were budding in my own armpits, growing, becoming darker and darker. . . .

Summer vacation arrived. Although I had looked forward to it impatiently, it proved to be one of those between-acts during which one does not know what to do with himself; although I had hungered for it, it proved to be an uneasy feast for me.

Ever since I had contracted a light case of tuberculosis in infancy, the doctor had forbidden me to expose myself to strong ultraviolet rays. When at the seacoast, I was never allowed to stay out in the direct rays of the sun more than thirty minutes at a time. Any violation of this rule always brought its own punishment in a swift attack of fever. I was not even allowed to take part in swimming practice at school. Consequently I had never learned to swim. Later, this inability to swim gained new significance in connection with the persistent fascination the sea came to have for me, with those occasions on which it exercised such turbulent power over me.

At the time of which I speak, however, I had not yet encountered this overpowering temptation of the sea. And yet, wanting somehow to while away the boredom of a season which was completely distasteful to me, a season moreover which awakened inexplicable longings within me, I spent that summer at the beach with my mother and brother and sister. . . .

Suddenly I realized that I had been left alone on the rock.

I had walked along the beach toward this rock with my brother and sister a short time before, looking for the tiny fish that flashed in the rivulets between the rocks. Our catch had not been as good as we had foreseen, and my small sister and brother had become bored. A maid had come to call us to the beach umbrella where my mother was sitting. I had refused crossly to turn back, and the maid had taken my brother and sister back with her, leaving me alone.

The sun of the summer afternoon was beating down incessantly upon the surface of the sea, and the entire bay was a single, stupendous expanse of glare. On the horizon some summer clouds were standing mutely still, half-immersing their magnificent, mournful, prophet-like forms in the sea. The muscles of the clouds were pale as alabaster.

A few sailboats and skiffs and several fishing boats had put out from the sandy beaches and were now moving about lazily upon the open sea. Except for the tiny figures in the boats, not a human form was to be seen. A subtle hush was over everything. As though a coquette had come telling her little secrets, a light breeze blew in from the sea, bringing to my ears a tiny sound like the invisible wing-beats of some lighthearted insects. The beach near me was made up almost altogether of low, docile rocks that tilted toward the sea. There were only two or three such jutting crags as this on which I was sitting.

From the offing the waves began and came sliding in over the surface of the sea in the form of restless green swells. Groups of low rocks extended out into the sea, where their resistance to the waves sent splashes high into the air, like white hands begging for help. The rocks were dipping themselves in the sea's sensation of deep abundance and seemed to be dreaming of buoys broken loose from their moorings. But in a flash the swell had passed them by and come sliding toward the beach with unabated speed. As it drew near the beach something awakened and rose up within its green hood. The wave grew tall and, as far as the eye could reach, revealed the razor-keen blade of the sea's enormous ax, poised and ready to strike. Suddenly the dark-blue guillotine fell, sending up a white blood-splash. The body of the wave, seething and falling, pursued its severed head, and for a moment it reflected the pure blue of the sky, that same unearthly blue which is mirrored in the eyes of a person on the verge of death. . . . During the brief instant of the wave's attack, the groups of rocks, smooth and eroded, had concealed themselves in white froth, but now, gradually emerging from the sea, they glittered in the retreating remnants of the wave. From the top of the rock where I sat watching, I could see hermit-shells sidling crazily across the glittering rocks and crabs become motionless in the glare.

All at once my feeling of solitude became mixed with memories of Omi. It was like this: My long-felt attraction toward the loneliness that filled Omi's life—loneliness born of the fact that life had enslaved him—had first made me want to possess the same quality; and now that I was experiencing, in this feeling of emptiness before the sea's repletion, a loneliness that outwardly resembled his, I wanted to savor it completely, through his very eyes. I would enact the double role of both

Omi and myself. But in order to do so I first had to discover some point of similarity with him, however slight. In that way I would be able to become a stand-in for Omi and consciously act exactly as though I were joyfully overflowing with that same loneliness which was probably only unconscious in him, attaining at last to a realization of that daydream in which the pleasure I felt at the sight of Omi became the pleasure Omi himself was feeling.

Ever since becoming obsessed with the picture of St. Sebastian, I had acquired the unconscious habit of crossing my hands over my head whenever I happened to be undressed. Mine was a frail body, without so much as a pale shadow of Sebastian's abundant beauty. But now once more I spontaneously fell into the pose. As I did so my eyes went to my armpits. And a mysterious sexual desire boiled up within me. . . .

Summer had come and, with it, there in my armpits, the first sprouts of black thickets, not the equal of Omi's it is true, but undoubtedly there. Here then was the point of similarity with Omi that my purposes required. There is no doubt that Omi himself was involved in my sexual desire, but neither could it be denied that this desire was directed mainly toward my own armpits. Urged on by a swarming combination of circumstances —the salt breeze that made my nostrils quiver, the strong summer sun that blazed down upon me and set my shoulders and chest to smarting, the absence of human form as far as the eye could reach—for the first time in my life I indulged in my "bad habit" out in the open, there beneath the blue sky. As its object I chose my own armpits. . . .

My body was shaken with a strange grief. I was on fire with a loneliness as fiery as the sun. My swimming trunks, made of navy-blue wool, were glued unpleasantly to my stomach. I climbed down slowly off the rock, stepping into a trapped pool of water at the edge of the beach. In the water my feet looked like white, dead shells, and down through it I could plainly see the bottom, studded with shells and flickering with ripples. I knelt down in the water and surrendered myself to a wave that broke at this moment and came rushing toward me with a violent roar. It struck me in the chest, almost burying me in its crushing whitecap. . . .

When the wave receded, my corruption had been washed away. Together with that receding wave, together with the countless living organisms it contained —microbes, seeds of marine plants, fish eggs—my myriad spermatozoa had been engulfed in the foaming sea and carried away.

When autumn came and the new school-term began, Omi was not there. A notice of his expulsion had been posted on the bulletin board.

All my classmates, without exception, immediately began chattering about Omi's misdeeds, acting like a populace after the death of a tyrant who had ruled over them:

"... He borrowed ten yen from me and then wouldn't pay it back.... He laughed as he robbed me of my imported fountain pen.... He almost strangled me...."

One after another they recounted the harms he had done them, until I seemed to be the only one who had never experienced his wickedness. I was mad with jealousy. My despair, however, was slightly assuaged by the fact that no one knew definitely why he had been expelled. Even those clever students who are always in the know at every school could not suggest a reason credible enough to find general acceptance. When we asked the teachers they of course would simply smile and say it was because of "something bad."

Only I, it appeared, had a secret conviction as to the nature of his "evil." I was sure that he had been participating in some vast conspiracy, which even he had not yet fully understood. The compulsion toward evil that some demon incited in him gave his life its meaning and constituted his destiny. At least so it seemed to me....

Upon further thought, however, his "evil" came to have a different meaning for me. I decided that the huge conspiracy into which the demon had driven him, with its intricately organized secret society and its minutely planned underground machinations, was surely all for the sake of some forbidden god. Omi had served that god, had attempted to convert others to his faith, had been betrayed, and then had been executed in secret. One evening at dusk he had been stripped naked and taken to the grove on the hill. There he had been bound to a tree, both hands tied high over his head. The first arrow had pierced the side of his chest; the second, his armpit.

The more I remembered the picture he had made that day, grasping the exercise-bar in preparation for the pull-up, the more I became convinced of his close affinity with St. Sebastian.

During my fourth year at middle school I developed anemia. I became even more pallid than usual, so much so that my hands were the color of dead grass. Whenever I climbed a steep staircase I had to squat down and rest at the top. I would feel as though a windspout of white fog had whirled down onto the back of my head, digging a hole there and making me all but faint away.

My family took me to the doctor, who diagnosed my trouble as anemia. He was an agreeable man and a friend of the family's. When they began asking him for details about my trouble, he said:

"Well, let's see what the answer book has to say about anemia."

The examination was over, and I was at the doctor's elbow, where I could peep into the book from which he began reading aloud. The family was seated facing him and could not see the pages of the book.

". . . So then, next there's the etiology—the causes of

the disease. Hookworms—these are a frequent cause. This is probably the boy's case. We'll have to have a stool examination. Next there's chlorosis. But it's rare, and anyway it's a woman's disease—"

At this point the book gave a further cause for anemia, but the doctor did not read it aloud. Instead, he skipped over it, mumbling the rest of the passage in his throat as he closed the book. But I had seen the phrase that he had omitted. It was "self-pollution."

I could feel my heart pounding with shame. The doctor had discovered my secret.

But what no one could ever have discovered was the singular reciprocal relationship between my lack of blood and my blood lust itself.

My inherent deficiency of blood had first implanted in me the impulse to dream of bloodshed. And in its turn that impulse had caused me to lose more and more of the stuff of blood from my body, thereby further increasing my lust for blood. This enfeebling life of dreaming sharpened and exercised my imagination. Although I was not yet acquainted with the works of De Sade, the description of the Colosseum in *Quo Vadis* had made a deep impression on me, and by myself I had dreamed up the idea of a murder theater.

There, in my murder theater, young Roman gladiators offered up their lives for my amusement; and all the deaths that took place there not only had to overflow with blood but also had to be performed with all due ceremony. I delighted in all forms of capital punishment and all implements of execution. But I would allow no torture devices nor gallows, as they would not have provided a spectacle of outpouring blood. Nor did I like explosive weapons, such as pistols or guns. So far as possible I chose primitive and savage weapons—arrows, daggers, spears. And in order to prolong the agony, it was the belly that must be aimed at. The sacrificial victim must send up long-drawn-out, mournful, pathetic cries, making the hearer feel the unutterable loneliness of existence. Thereupon my joy of life, blazing up from some secret place deep within me, would finally give its own shout of exultation, answering the victim cry for cry. Was this not exactly similar to the joy ancient man found in the hunt?

The weapon of my imagination slaughtered many a Grecian soldier, many white slaves of Arabia, princes of savage tribes, hotel elevator-boys, waiters, young toughs, army officers, circus roustabouts. . . . I was one of those savage marauders who, not knowing how to express their love, mistakenly kill the persons they love. I would kiss the lips of those who had fallen to the ground and were still moving spasmodically.

From some allusion or other I had conceived an instrument of execution contrived in such a way that a thick board studded with scores of upright daggers, arranged in the shape of a human figure, would come sliding down a rail upon a cross of execution fixed to the other side of the rail. There was an execution factory where mechanical drills for piercing the human body were always running, where the blood juice was sweetened, canned, and put on the market. Within the head of this middle-school student innumerable victims were bound with their hands behind them and escorted to the Colosseum.

The impulse gradually grew stronger within me, arriving one day at a daydream that was probably one of the basest of which man is capable. As with my other daydreams, here again the victim was one of my own classmates, a skilled swimmer, with a notably good physique.

It was in a cellar. A clandestine banquet was being held. Elegant candlesticks gleamed above a pure-white tablecloth; there was an array of silver cutlery flanking each plate. There were even the usual bouquets of carnations. But it was curious that the blank space in the center of the table should be so excessively large. Surely it would be an extremely large platter which was to be brought in and placed there.

"Not yet?" one of the guests asked me. His face was in the shadow and could not be seen. His solemn voice sounded like that of an aged man.

Now that I think of it, shadows hid the faces of all the diners. Only their white hands extended into the light, where they toyed with silver-shining knives and forks. An endless murmuring hung in the air, sounding like a group of people talking together in low voices, or talking to themselves. It was a funereal feast; the only sound that could be plainly heard was the occasional creaking or grating of a chair.

"It ought to be ready soon," I answered.

Again the gloomy silence fell. I could clearly sense that everyone was displeased with my answer.

"Shall I go and see?"

I got up and opened the door into the kitchen. In one corner of the kitchen there was a stone staircase leading up to street-level.

"Not yet?" I asked the cook.

"What? Oh, in just a minute." The cook answered without looking up from his work, as though he too were out of humor. He was chopping up some sort of salad greens. On the kitchen table there was nothing but a thick plank about three feet wide and almost twelve feet long.

A sound of laughter came down the stone stairwell. I looked up and saw a second cook come down the stairs leading this young muscular classmate of mine by the arm. The boy was wearing slacks and a dark-blue polo shirt that left his chest bare.

"Ah, it's B, isn't it?" I said to him offhand.

When he reached the bottom of the stairs he stood nonchalantly, not taking his hands from his pockets. Turning to me, he began to laugh jokingly. Just at that moment one of the cooks sprang upon him from the rear and got a strangle hold around his neck.

The boy struggled violently.

As I watched his piteous struggles, I told myself: "It's a judo hold—yes, that's it, it's some judo hold, but what's the name of it? That's right, strangle him again—he couldn't be really dead yet—he's just fainted—"

Suddenly the boy's head hung limp within the crook of the cook's massive arm. Then the cook picked the boy up carelessly in his arms and dropped him on the kitchen table. The other cook went to the table and began working over the boy with business-like hands; he stripped off the boy's polo shirt, removed his wrist watch, took off his trousers, and had him stark naked in an instant.

The naked youth lay where he had fallen, face up on the table, his lips slightly parted. I gave those lips a lingering kiss.

"How shall it be—face up or face down?" the cook asked me.

"Face up, I suppose," I answered, thinking to myself that in that position the boy's chest would be visible, looking like an amber-colored shield.

The other cook took a large foreign-style platter down from a rack and brought it to the table. It was exactly the size for holding a human body and was curiously made, with five small holes cut through the rim on either side.

"Heave ho!" the two cooks said in unison, lifting the unconscious boy and laying him face-up on the platter. Then, whistling merrily, they passed a cord through the holes on both sides of the dish, lashing the boy's body down securely. Their nimble hands moved expertly at the task. They arranged some large salad leaves prettily around the naked body and placed an unusually large steel carving knife and fork on the platter.

"Heave ho!" they said again, lifting the platter onto their shoulders. I opened the door into the dining-room for them.

We were greeted by a welcoming silence. The platter was put down, filling that blank space on the table, which had been glittering blankly in the light. Returning to my seat, I lifted the large knife and fork from the platter and said:

"Where shall I begin?"

There was no answer. One could sense rather than see many faces craning forward toward the platter.

"This is probably a good spot to begin on." I thrust the fork upright into the heart. A fountain of blood struck me full in the face. Holding the knife in my right hand, I began carving the flesh of the breast, gently, thinly at first. . . .

Even after my anemia was cured, my bad habit only grew the worse. The youngest of my teachers was the geometry instructor. I never tired of looking at his face during class. He had a complexion that had been burned by the seaside sun, a sonorous voice like a fisherman's. I had heard that he had formerly been a swimming coach.

One winter day in geometry class I was copying into my notebook from the blackboard, keeping one hand in my pants pocket. Presently my eyes strayed unconsciously from my work and began following the instructor. He was getting on and off the platform while, in his youthful voice, he repeated the explanation of a difficult problem.

Pangs of sex had already been intruding upon my everyday life. Now, before my eyes, the young instructor gradually changed into a vision of a statue of the nude Hercules. He had been cleaning the blackboard, holding an eraser in his left hand and chalk in the other; then, still erasing, he stretched out his right hand and began writing an equation on the board. As he did so the wrinkles that gathered in the material at the back of his coat were, to my bemused eyes, the muscle-furrows of "Hercules Drawing the Bow." And at last I had committed my bad habit there in the midst of schoolwork. . . .

The signal for recess sounded. I hung my dazed head and followed the others onto the playground. The boy with whom I was then in love—this also was an unrequited love, another student who had failed his examinations—came up to me and asked:

"Hey, you, didn't you finally go to Katakura's house yesterday? How was it?"

Katakura had been a quiet classmate of ours who had died of tuberculosis. His funeral services had ended two days before. As I had heard from a friend that his face was completely changed in death and looked like the face of an evil spirit, I had waited to make my call of condolence until I was sure his body had been cremated.

I could think of no reply to my friend's sudden question and said curtly:

"There was nothing to it. But then he was already ashes." Suddenly I remembered a message which would flatter him. "Oh, yes, and Katakura's mother told me over and over again to be sure and give you her regards." I giggled meaninglessly. "She asked me to tell you by all means to come to see her, because she'll be lonesome now."

"Aw, go on!" And suddenly a blow on the chest took me by surprise. Although delivered with full force, his blow was still charged with friendliness. His cheeks had become crimson with embarrassment, as though he were still a child. I saw that his eyes were shining with an unaccustomed intimacy, seeming to regard me as his accomplice in something.

"Go on!" he said again, "haven't you become dirty minded! You and your way of laughing!"

For a moment I did not grasp his meaning. I smiled lamely and for a full thirty seconds failed to understand him. Then I caught on: Katakura's mother was a widow, still young, with a lovely slender figure.

I felt miserable. It was not so much because my slowness in comprehending could only have arisen from stupidity, but rather because the incident had revealed such an obvious difference between his focus of interest and my own. I felt the emptiness of the gulf that separated us, and was filled with mortification at having been surprised by such a belated discovery of something I ought naturally to have foreseen. I had given him the message from Katakura's mother without stopping to consider what his reaction would be, simply knowing unconsciously that here I had a chance to curry favor with him. Now I was appalled by the ugly sight of my callowness, as ugly as the streaks of dried tears on a child's face.

On this occasion I was too exhausted to ask myself the question I had asked so many thousands of times before: Why is it wrong for me to stay just the way I am now? I was fed up with myself and, for all my chastity, was ruining my body. I had thought that with "earnestness" (what a touching thought!) I too could escape from my childish state. It was as though I had not yet realized that what I was now disgusted with was my true self, was clearly a part of my true life; it was as though I believed instead that these had been years of dreaming, from which I would now turn to "real life."

I was feeling the urge to begin living. To begin living my true life? Even if it was to be pure masquerade and not my life at all, still the time had come when I must make a start, must drag my heavy feet forward.

CHAPTER THREE

Everyone says that life is a stage. But most people do not seem to become obsessed with the idea, at any rate not as early as I did. By the end of childhood I was already firmly convinced that it was so and that I was to play my part on the stage without once ever revealing my true self. Since my conviction was accompanied by an extremely naïve lack of experience, even though there was a lingering suspicion somewhere in my mind that I might be mistaken, I was still practically certain that all men embarked on life in just this way. I believed optimistically that once the performance was finished the curtain would fall and the audience would never see the actor without his make-up. My assumption that I would die young was also a factor in this belief. In the course of time, however, this optimism or, better said, this daydream was to suffer a cruel disillusionment.

By way of precaution I should add that it is not the usual matter of "self-consciousness" to which I am referring here. Instead it is simply a matter of sex, of the role by means of which one attempts to conceal, often even from himself, the true nature of his sexual desires. For the present I do not intend to refer to anything beyond that.

Now it may well be that the so-called backward student is the product of heredity. I nevertheless wanted to receive regular promotions along with the rest of my generation in the school of life, and I hit upon a makeshift way of doing so. This device consisted, in brief, of copying my friends' answers during examinations, without any understanding of what I was writing, and handing in my paper with studied innocence. There are times when such a method, more stupid and shameless than cunning, reaps an outward success, and the pupil is promoted. In the grade to which he has advanced, however, he is presumed to have mastered the materials of the lower grades, and as the lessons progress in difficulty, he becomes completely lost. Even though he hears what the teacher says, he understands not a word of it. At this point only two courses are open to him: either he goes to the dogs, or else he bluffs his way through by pretending with all his might that he does understand. The choice between these two courses will be determined by the nature, not the quantity, of his weakness and boldness. Either course requires the same amount of boldness, or of weakness, and either requires a kind of lyrical and imperishable craving for laziness.

One day I joined a group of classmates who were walking along outside the school walls, noisily discussing the rumor that one of our friends, who was not present, had fallen in love with the conductress of a bus on which he went back and forth to school. Before long the gossip turned to a theoretical argument as to what one could find to like about bus conductresses.

At this point I spoke up, deliberately adopting a cold-blooded tone and speaking brusquely, as though flinging out the words:

"It's their uniforms! Because they fit so tight to their bodies."

Needless to say, I had never felt the slightest such sensual attraction toward bus conductresses as my words suggested. I had spoken by analogy—a perfect analogy, in which I saw the same sort of tight uniform on a different body—and also out of a desire, then very strong in me, to pose as a mature, cynical sensualist about everything.

The other boys reacted immediately. They were all of that type known as "honor students," of unimpeachable deportment, and—as was so often the case at my school—correspondingly prudish. Their shocked disapproval of my words was clear from their half-joking remarks:

"Ugh! You know all about it, don't you?"

"Nobody'd dream of such a thing unless he'd been doing a lot he shouldn't."

"Hey, you're really awful, aren't you?"

Encountering such naïve, excited criticism, I feared my medicine had been a bit too effective. I reflected that I could probably have shown my profundity off to better advantage if, even in saying the same thing, I had used a little less sophisticated and startling way of speaking, that I ought to have been more reserved.

When a boy of fourteen or fifteen discovers that he is more given to introspection and consciousness of self than other boys his age, he easily falls into the error of believing it is because he is more mature than they. This was certainly a mistake in my case. Rather it was because the other boys had no such need of understanding themselves as I had: they could be their natural selves, whereas I was to play a part, a fact that would require considerable understanding and study. So it was not my maturity but my sense of uneasiness, my uncertainty, that was forcing me to gain control over my consciousness. Because such consciousness was simply a steppingstone to aberration, and my present thinking was nothing but uncertain and haphazard guesswork.

My uneasiness was the same as that of which Stephan Zweig speaks when he says that "what we call evil is the instability inherent in all mankind which drives man outside and beyond himself toward an unfathomable something, exactly as though Nature had bequeathed to our souls an ineradicable portion of instability from her store of ancient chaos." This legacy of unrest produces strain and "attempts to resolve itself back into super-human and super-sensory elements." So then, it was this same instability that drove me on, while the other boys, having no need for self-awareness, could dispense with introspection.

Bus conductresses possessed not the slightest sexual attraction for me, and yet I saw that my words, spoken deliberately both because of the analogy and the other considerations I have mentioned, had not only actually shocked my friends and made them blush with embarrassment, but had also played upon their adolescent susceptibility to suggestive ideas and produced an obscure sexual excitement in them. At this sight, a spiteful feeling of superiority naturally arose in me.

But my feelings did not stop there. Now it was my own turn to be deceived. I sobered up from my feeling of superiority, but distortedly, one-sidedly. The process was like this:

One part of my feeling of superiority became conceit, became the intoxication of considering myself a step ahead of mankind. Then, when this intoxicated part became sober more swiftly than the rest, I committed the rash error of judging everything with my sobered consciousness, not taking into consideration the fact that part of me was still drunk. Therefore the intoxicating thought of "I am ahead of others" was amended to the diffidence of "No, I too am a human being like the rest." Because of the miscalculation, this in turn was amplified into "And also I am a human being like them *in every respect.*" The part of me that was not yet sober made such an amplification possible and supported it. And at last I arrived at the conceited conclusion that "Everyone is like me." The way of thinking that I have called a steppingstone to aberration came powerfully into play in reaching this conclusion. . . .

Thus I had succeeded in hypnotizing myself. And from that time on, ninety percent of my life came to be governed by this autohypnosis, this irrational, idiotic, counterfeit hypnosis, which even I definitely knew to be counterfeit. It may well be wondered if there has ever been a person more given to credulity.

Will the reader understand? There was a very simple reason why I had been able to use even the slightest of sensual words when speaking of bus conductresses. And this was the very point I had failed to perceive. . . . It was truly a simple reason—nothing more than that, where women were concerned, I was devoid of that shyness which other boys possess innately.

In order to escape the charge that I am simply crediting the person I was in those days with powers of judgment I did not possess until today, let me cite here a passage from something I wrote at the age of fifteen:

... Ryotaro lost no time in making himself a part of this new circle of friends. He believed confidently that he could conquer his reasonless melancholy and ennui by being—or pretending to be—even a little cheerful. Credulity, the acme of belief, had left him in a state of incandescent repose. Whenever he joined in some mean jest or prank he always told himself: "Now I'm not blue, now I'm not bored." He styled this "forgetting troubles."

Most people are always doubtful as to whether they are happy or not, cheerful or not. This is the normal state of happiness, as doubt is a most natural thing.

Ryotaro alone declares "I am happy," and convinces himself that it is true.

Because of this, people are inclined to believe in his so-called "unquestionable happiness." And at last a faint but real thing is confined in a powerful machine of falsehood. The machine sets to work mightily. And people do not even notice that he is a mass of "self-deceit." ...

"... The machine sets to work mightily...." Was it not actually working mightily in my case?

It is a common failing of childhood to think that if one makes a hero out of a demon the demon will be satisfied.

So then, the time had come when somehow or other I had to make a start in life. The supply of knowledge with which I was equipped for the journey consisted of little more than the many novels I had read, a sex encyclopedia for home use, the pornography that passed from hand to hand among the students, and an abundance of naïve dirty jokes heard from friends on nights of field exercises. Finally, even more important than all these, there was also the burning curiosity that would be my faithful traveling companion. To begin my journey I had to take a posture of departure at the gate, and for this the determination to be "a machine of falsehood" was sufficient.

I studied many novels minutely, investigating how boys my age felt about life, how they spoke to themselves. I was cut off from dormitory life; I took no part in school athletics; moreover, my school was full of little snobs who, once outgrowing that meaningless game of Dirty which I have described, rarely had anything to do with vulgar matters; and to top it all, I was extremely bashful. All of these facts taken together made it difficult for me to know the psychology of any of my schoolmates. As a result, my only recourse was to infer from theoretical rules what "a boy my age" would feel when he was all alone.

The period called adolescence—I had my full share of it so far as burning curiosity was concerned—seemed to have come to pay us a sick visit. Having attained puberty, the boys seemed to do nothing but always think immoderately about women, exude pimples, and write sugary verses out of heads that were in a constant dizzy reel. They had read, first this study of sex, which emphasized the harmful effects of masturbation, and then that, which spoke reassuringly of no great harmful effects; as a result, they too appeared to have finally become enthusiastic practitioners. Here was another point, I told myself, where I am *completely identical* with them. In my state of autohypnosis I overlooked the fact that, in spite of the identical nature of the physical action, there was a profound difference so far as its mental objects were concerned.

The principal difference was the fact that the other boys seemed to derive unusual excitement from the mere word woman. They always blushed if the word so much as floated through their minds. I, on the other hand, received no more sensual impression from "woman" than from "pencil," or "automobile," or "broom." Even in my conversation with friends I often manifested a similar deficiency in the faculty of associating ideas, as in the incident concerning Katakura's mother, and made remarks that sounded altogether incoherent to them. My friends solved this puzzle to their satisfaction by considering me a poet. But for my part I definitely did not want to be thought a poet: I had heard that members of the breed of men called poets were invariably jilted by women. So in order to make my conversation consistent with my friends', I cultivated an artificial ability to make the same association of ideas as they.

I never guessed that they could be sharply distinguished from me, not only in their inner feelings, but even in hidden external signs. I did not realize, in short, that they immediately had an erection when they saw a picture of a woman's nude body, that I was alone in remaining unmoved at such a time. Nor did I realize that an object that would incite an erection in my case (strangely enough, from the very first such objects were confined to that class of things which are the character-istic sexual objects of inversion), say a statue of a naked youth cast in the Ionian mold, would not have excited them in the slightest.

My purpose in having given a detailed description of several instances of erection in the preceding chapter was to make more understandable this important point of my ignorance concerning myself. Because my lack of knowledge as to the objects that excited other boys served to strengthen the autohypnosis of considering myself to be like them. Where could I have obtained enlightenment? Novels abound in kissing scenes, but none that I had read made any reference to such a thing as erections on such occasions. This was only natural, as it is scarely a subject to be described in a novel. But even the sex encyclopedia said nothing concerning erec-tion as a physiological accompaniment of the kiss, leav-ing me instead with the impression that erection occur-red only as prelude to carnal relations or in response to a mental picture of the act. I thought that when the time came, even if there were to be no desire, I too would suddenly have an erection, exactly as though it were an inspiration from beyond the skies. A small something deep inside me continued whispering: "No, maybe in your case alone it will not happen." And this small doubt was manifested in all my feelings of insecurity.

But at the moment of indulging in my bad habit did I never even once picture to myself some part of a woman? Not even experimentally? No, never. I explained this strange lapse to myself as being due simply to my laziness.

In short, I knew absolutely nothing about other boys. I did not know that each night all boys but me had dreams in which women—women barely glimpsed yesterday on a street corner—were stripped of their clothing and set one by one to parading before the dreamers' eyes. I did not know that in the boys' dreams the breasts of a woman would often float up like beautiful jellyfish rising from the sea of night. I did not know that in those dreams the precious part of a woman would open its moist lips and keep singing a siren's melody, tens of times, hundreds of times, thousands of times, eternally. . . .

Was it out of laziness that I had no such dreams? Could it have been because of laziness? I kept asking myself. All of my earnestness toward life as a whole arose out of this suspicion that I was simply lazy. And in the end this earnestness spent itself in defending myself against the charge of laziness on this one point, insuring that my laziness could remain laziness still.

This earnestness led me in the first place to resolve to gather together all my memories concerning women, starting back at the very beginning. What an extremely meager collection it turned out to be!

I remembered one incident that had taken place when I was about thirteen or fourteen. It was the day of my father's transfer to Osaka, and we had all gone to Tokyo Station to see him off. Afterwards, a number of relatives had returned to the house with us. Among them was my second cousin Sumiko, an unmarried girl of about twenty.

Sumiko's front teeth protruded the tiniest bit. They were exceedingly white and beautiful teeth, and when she laughed they gleamed so brightly that one wondered whether she was not laughing on purpose to show them off. Their slight appearance of prominence added a subtle attractiveness to her smile; in her case the defect of protruding teeth was like a pinch of spice dropped into the harmonious grace and beauty of her face and figure, emphasizing the harmony and adding an accent of flavor to the beauty.

If the word "love" is not applicable, at least I "liked" this cousin. Ever since childhood I had enjoyed watching her from a distance. I would sit beside her for hours as she embroidered, doing nothing but stare at her vacantly.

After a time my aunts went into an inner room, leaving Sumiko and me alone in the parlor. We remained just as we were, seated side by side on a sofa, saying nothing. Our heads were still buzzing with the bustle of the station platform. I felt unusually weary.

"Oh, I'm tired," she said, giving a little yawn. She lifted her white hand wearily and tapped her mouth lightly several times with her white fingers, as though performing some superstitious ritual. "Aren't you tired too, Kochan?"

For some unknown reason, as she said this she covered her face with both sleeves of her kimono and buried it with a plop upon my thigh. Then, rolling her cheek slowly against my trousers, she turned her face up and remained motionless for a time.

The trousers of my uniform trembled at the honor of serving as her pillow. The fragrance of her perfume and powder confused me. I looked upon her unmoving profile as she lay there with her tired, clear eyes wide open; I was at a loss. . . .

That is all that happened. And yet I never forgot the feeling of that luxurious weight pressing for a moment upon my thigh. It was not a sexual feeling, but somehow simply an extremely luxurious pleasure, like that feeling produced by the weight of a decoration hanging on the breast.

I often encountered an anemic young lady on the buses I took to school. Her cold attitude caught my interest. She always stared distinterestedly out the window as though very bored with everything, and as she did so, the willfulness of her slightly pouting lips was striking. When she was not on the bus, something seemed to be missing, and before I realized it I was breathlessly hoping to see her every time I got on the bus.

I wondered if this could be what was called love. I simply did not know. I had not the faintest idea that there was any connection between love and sexual desire. Needless to say, during the time of my infatuation with Omi I had made no effort to apply the word love to that diabolical fascination he exercised over me. And now again, even while I was wondering if the vague emotion I was feeling toward the girl on the bus could be love, at the same instant I could feel attracted to the rough young bus-driver, his hair gleaming with heavy pomade.

My ignorance was so profound that I did not perceive the contradiction involved here. I did not see that in my way of looking at the profile of the young bus-driver there was something inevitable, suffocating, painful, oppressive, whereas it was with rather studied, artificial, and easily tired eyes that I regarded the anemic young lady. So long as I remained unaware of the difference in these two viewpoints, both of them lived together within me without bothering each other, without any conflict.

For a boy of my age I seem to have been singularly uninterested in what is called "moral cleanliness" or, to use another phrase, to have been lacking the talent for "self-control." Even if I could explain this fact by saying that my excessively intense curiosity did not naturally dispose me toward an interest in morality, there would still remain the fact that this curiosity of mine both resembled the hopeless yearnings of a bedridden invalid for the outside world and was also somehow inextricably tangled up with a belief in the possibility of the impossible. It was this combination—one part unconscious belief, one part unconscious despair—that so quickened my desires that they appeared to be desperate ambitions.

Even though still young, I did not know what it was to experience the clear-cut feeling of platonic love. Was this a misfortune? But what meaning could ordinary misfortune have for me? The vague uneasiness surrounding my sexual feelings had practically made the carnal world an obsession with me. My curiosity was actually purely intellectual, not far removed from the desire for knowledge, but I became skillful at convincing myself that it was carnal desire incarnate. What is more, I mastered the art of delusion until I could regard myself as a truly lewd-minded person. As a result I assumed the stylish airs of an adult, of a man of the world. I affected the attitude of being completely tired of women.

Thus it was that I first became obsessed with the idea of the kiss. Actually the action called a kiss represented nothing more for me than some place where my spirit could seek shelter. I can say so now. But at that time, in order to delude myself that this desire was animal passion, I had to undertake an elaborate disguise of my true self. The unconscious feeling of guilt resulting from this false pretense stubbornly insisted that I play a conscious and false role.

But, it may well be asked, can a person be so completely false to his own nature? even for one moment? If the answer is no, then there is no way to explain the mysterious mental process by which we crave things we actually do not want at all, is there? If it is granted that I was the exact opposite of the ethical man who suppresses his immoral desires, does this mean my heart was cherishing the most immoral desires? In any case, were my desires not exceedingly petty? Or had I deceived myself completely? was I actually acting in every last detail as a slave of convention? . . . The time was to come when I could no longer shirk the necessity of finding answers to these questions. . . .

With the beginning of the war a wave of hypocritical stoicism swept the entire country. Even the higher schools did not escape: all during middle school we had longed for that happy day of graduation to higher school when we could let our hair grow long, but now, when the day arrived, we were no longer allowed to gratify our ambition—we still had to shave our heads. The craze for gaudy socks was likewise a thing of the past. Instead, periods of military drill became absurdly frequent and various other ridiculous innovations were undertaken.

Thanks, however, to our school's long practice at giving an adroit but mere outward appearance of conformity, we were able to continue our school life without being particularly affected by the new restrictions. The colonel assigned to the school by the War Ministry was an understanding man, and even the warrant officer whom we had nicknamed Mr. Zu because of his countrified way of pronouncing "su" as "zu," as well as his colleagues Mr. Booby and the pug-nosed Mr. Snout, got the hang of our school spirit and fell in with it sensibly enough. Our principal was a womanish old admiral, and with the support of the Imperial Household Ministry, he kept his position by following a dawdling and inoffensive principle of moderation in all things.

During this time I learned to smoke and drink. That is to say, I learned to make a pretense at smoking and drinking. The war had produced a strangely sentimental maturity in us. It arose from our thinking of life as something that would end abruptly in our twenties; we never even considered the possibility of there being anything beyond those few remaining years. Life struck us as being a strangely volatile thing. It was exactly as though life were a salt lake from which most of the water had suddenly evaporated, leaving such a heavy concentration of salt that our bodies floated buoyantly upon its surface. Since the moment for the curtain to fall was not so far distant, it might have been expected that I would enact with all the more diligence the masquerade I had devised for myself. But even while telling myself that I would start tomorrow—tomorrow for sure—my journey into life was postponed day after day, and the war years were going by without the slightest sign of my departure.

Was this not a unique period of happiness for me? Though I still felt an uneasiness, it was only faint; still having hope, I looked forward to the unknown blue skies of each tomorrow. Fanciful dreams of the journey to come, visions of its adventure, the mental picture of the somebody I would one day become in the world and of the lovely bride I had not yet seen, my hopes of fame—in those days all these things were neatly arranged in a trunk against the moment of my departure, exactly like a traveler's guidebooks, towel, toothbrush, and tooth paste. I found childish delight in war, and despite the presence of death and destruction all around me, there was no abatement of the daydream in which I believed myself beyond the reach of harm by any bullet. I even shuddered with a strange delight at the thought of my own death. I felt as though I owned the whole world. And little wonder, because at no time are we ever in such complete possession of a journey, down to its last nook and cranny, as when we are busy with preparations for it. After that, there remains only the journey itself, which is nothing but the process through which we lose our ownership of it. This is what makes travel so utterly fruitless.

In time my obsession with the idea of kissing became fixed upon a single pair of lips. Even here I was probably inspired by nothing more than a desire to give my dreams pretensions to a nobler pedigree. As I have already suggested, although I actually experienced neither desire nor any other emotion in regard to those lips, I nevertheless tried desperately to convince myself that I did desire them. In short, I was mistaking as primary desire something that actually was only the irrational and secondary desire of wanting to believe I desired them. I was mistaking the fierce, impossible desire of not wanting to be myself for the sexual desire of a man of the world, for the desire that arises from his being himself.

At that time I had a friend with whom I was on intimate terms even though we were not in the least compatible, not even in our conversation. This was a frivolous classmate named Nukada. He seemed to have chosen me as a readily agreeable partner with whom he could be at ease while asking various questions about first-year German lessons, with which he was having great difficulty. As I am always enthusiastic about a new thing until its newness is gone, I gave the appearance of being an excellent German student, though only during that first year. Nukada must have realized intuitively how much I secretly detested the label of honor student that I had been given and how I longed for a "bad reputation." Honor student—I told myself it was a label that would better become a theology major, and yet I could find no other that would provide me with better camouflage. Nukada's friendship contained something that appealed to this weak point of mine—because he was the object of much jealousy on the part of the "tough boys" in our school; because through him I caught faint echoes of communications from the world of women, in exactly the same way that one communicates with the spirit world through a medium.

Omi had been the first medium between me and the world of women. But at that time I had been more my natural self, and so had been content to count his special qualifications as a medium as but a part of his beauty. Nukada's role as a medium, however, became the supernatural framework for my curiosity. This was probably due, at least in part, to the fact that Nukada was not at all beautiful.

The lips that had become my obsession were those of Nukada's elder sister, whom I saw when I went to visit at his house. It was easy for this beautiful girl of twenty-three to treat me as a child. By watching the men who surrounded her, I came to realize that I possessed not a single trait that could attract a woman. Thus, at long last, I admitted to myself that I could never become an Omi and, upon further consideration, that my desire to become like Omi had in fact been love for Omi.

And yet I was still convinced that I was in love with Nukada's sister. Acting exactly like any other inexperienced higher-school student of my age, I hung about the neighborhood of her house, patiently passing long hours at a nearby bookshop, hoping for a chance of stopping her if she should pass; I hugged a cushion and imagined the feeling of embracing her, drew countless pictures of her lips, and talked to myself as though out of my mind. And what was the good of it all? Those artificial efforts only inflicted some strange, numbed tiredness upon my mind. The realistic portion of my mind sensed the artificiality in the eternal protestations with which I persuaded myself that I was in love with her, and it fought back with this spiteful fatigue. There seemed to be some terrible poison in this mental exhaustion.

Between the intervals of these mental efforts I was making toward artificiality I would sometimes be overwhelmed with a paralyzing emptiness and, in order to escape, would turn shamelessly to a different sort of daydream. Then immediately I would become quick with life, would become myself, and would blaze toward strange images. Moreover, the flame thus created would remain in my mind as an abstract feeling, divorced from the reality of the image that had caused it, and I would distort my interpretation of the feeling until I believed it to be evidence of passion inspired by the girl herself. . . . Thus once again I deceived myself.

If there are those who would reproach me, saying that what I have been describing is too much of a generalization, too abstract, I can only reply that I have had no intention of giving a tedious description of a period of my life whose outward aspects differed in no way from those of normal adolescence. Excepting the shameful portion of my mind, my adolescence was, even in its inner aspects, altogether ordinary, and during that period I was exactly like any other boy. The reader need only picture to himself a fairly good student, not yet twenty; with average curiosity and average appetite for life; of a retiring disposition probably for no other reason than that he is too much given to introspection; quick to blush at the slightest word; and, lacking the confidence that comes from being handsome enough to appeal to girls, clinging perforce only to his books. It will be quite enough to picture to oneself how that student yearns for women, how his breast is afire, and how he is in useless agony.

Can there be anything more prosaic or easy to imagine? It is right that I should omit these tedious details, which would only repeat what everyone already knows. Suffice it to say, then, that—always excepting the one shameful difference I am describing—in that most colorless phase of the bashful student I was exactly like the other boys, that I had sworn unconditional loyalty to the stage manager of the play called adolescence.

During this time the attraction I had formerly felt only toward older youths had little by little been extended to include younger boys as well. This was only natural as by this time even these younger boys were the same age Omi had been when I was in love with him. But this transference of my love to persons in a different age group was also related to a more fundamenal change in the nature of my love. Just as before, I kept this new feeling hidden in my heart, but to my love for the savage there had now been added a love for the graceful and gentle. Along with my natural growth there was developing in me something like a guardian's love, something akin to boy-love.

Hirschfeld divides inverts into two categories: *androphils,* who are attracted only by adults; and *ephebophils,* who are fond of youths between the ages of fourteen and twenty-one. I was coming to understand the feelings of the ephebophils. In ancient Greece a young man was called an ephebe from the age of eighteen to twenty, while receiving military training; the term is derived from the same Greek word appearing in the name of Hebe, daughter of Zeus and Hera, cupbearer to the gods on Olympus, wife of the immortal Hercules, and symbol of the springtime of life.

There was a beautiful boy, not yet seventeen, who had just entered higher school. He had a light complexion, gentle lips, and perfectly curved eyebrows. I had learned that his name was Yakumo. His features appealed to me greatly.

Without his being aware of it, he began presenting

me with a series of gifts, each consisting of a full week of pleasure. The section monitors of the senior class, of whom I was one, gave commands by weekly turns at morning assembly, morning calisthenics, and afternoon drill. (This latter, as required in higher school in those days, consisted of about thirty minutes of naval gymnastics, after which we would shoulder tools and go to dig air-raid trenches or to mow grass.) My turn for giving commands came around every fourth week. Even our school, for all its fastidious ways, appeared to be succumbing to the rude fashions of the times, and with the arrival of summer we were ordered to strip to the waist both for morning exercises and for naval gymnastics in the afternoon.

The order of events was for the monitor first to give the commands for morning assembly from the platform. Then when assembly was over he would give the command "Jackets off!" After everyone had started stripping, he would come down and stand at one side of the formation. Then he would give the order for the students to bow to the gymnastics instructor, who had taken his place on the platform. At this point the monitor's job was finished, as the instructor directed the exercises, so he would run back to the last row of his section, where he too would strip to the waist and join in the exercises.

I dreaded having to give commands so much that the mere thought made me feel chill, and yet the stiff military formality of the ceremony provided me with such a rare opportunity that I somehow looked forward to the week when my turn would come: thanks to it, Yakumo's body, Yakumo's half-naked body, was placed directly before my eyes, and without the danger of his seeing my unlovely nakedness.

As a rule Yakumo stood immediately in front of the platform, in the first or second row. His hyacinthine cheeks flushed readily, and I delighted in seeing them, puffing slightly, when he would come running to assembly and take his place in line. Gasping for breath, he would always unfasten the hooks on his blouse with rough movements. Then he would jerk his shirttail violently from his trousers as though to rip it to shreds.

Even when I was determined not to look at him, from my place on the platform I found it impossible to keep my gaze off his smooth, white body when it was thus exposed to public view with such indifference. (Once my blood was frozen by a friend's innocent remark: "You always keep your eyes lowered when you're giving commands from the platform—are you really that chickenhearted?") But on these occasions I had no chance to get closer to his rosy half-nakedness.

Then in the summer all the upper classes went for a week of study and observation at a naval engineering school at M. One day while there, we were all taken to swim in the pool. Rather than admit that I could not swim, I begged off on the pretext of having an upset stomach. I had expected to remain a mere spectator. But then some captain said sunbathing was medicine for any illness, and even those of us who had claimed to be too sick to swim were made to strip to our shorts.

Suddenly I noticed Yakumo was one of our group. He was lying with his white, muscular arms folded, exposing his lightly tanned chest to the breeze, and steadily chewing his lower lip as though teasing it with his white teeth. The self-styled invalids had begun to gather in the shade of a tree beside the pool, and I had no difficulty in drawing near him. Sitting beside him, I measured his slim waist with my eye and gazed at his gently breathing abdomen. As I did so I recalled a line from Whitman:

> *The young men float on their backs—their*
> *white bellies bulge to the sun . . .*

But now again I said not a word. I was ashamed of my own thin chest, of my bony, pallid arms. . . .

In September, 1944, the year before the end of the war, I graduated from the school I had attended ever since childhood and entered a certain university. Given no other choice by my father, I entered the Law Department. But I was not greatly annoyed by this as I was convinced that I would soon be called into the army and would die in battle, and that my family also would mercifully be killed in the air raids, leaving not a single survivor.

As was the common practice in those days, I borrowed a university uniform from an upperclassman who was going to war just when I was matriculating, promising to return it to his family when I myself should be called up. I put on the uniform and began going to classes.

The air raids were becoming more frequent. I was uncommonly afraid of them, and yet at the same time I somehow looked forward to death impatiently, with a sweet expectation. As I have remarked several times, the future was a heavy burden for me. From the very beginning, life had oppressed me with a heavy sense of duty. Even though I was clearly incapable of performing this duty, life still nagged at me for my dereliction. Thus I longed for the great sense of relief that death would surely bring if only, like a wrestler, I could wrench the heavy weight of life from my shoulders. I sensuously accepted the creed of death that was popular during the war. I thought that if by any chance I should attain "glorious death in battle" (how ill it would have become me!), this would be a truly ironical end for my life, and I could laugh sarcastically at it forever from the grave. . . . And when the sirens sounded, that same me would dash for the air-raid shelters faster than anyone. . . .

I heard the sound of a piano, clumsily played.

It was at the home of a friend who had decided to volunteer shortly as a special cadet. His name was Kusano, and I thought highly of him, regarding him as the only friend I had had in higher school with whom I could talk even slightly of serious matters. Indeed I still value his friendship today. I am a person who has no particular desire to have friends, but I am made miserable by something inside me that forces me to tell what follows, even though it is quite likely to destroy the sole friendship I have.

"Does whoever's playing that piano show promise? Sometimes the playing sounds a little uneven, doesn't it?"

"That's my sister. Her teacher's just gone and she's reviewing the lesson."

We ceased talking and listened intently. As Kusano's enlistment was close at hand, it was probably not just the sound of the piano in the next room that rang in his ears but rather a familiar, everyday thing, a kind of clumsy, irritating beauty, that he would soon have to leave behind. In the tonal color of those piano sounds there was a feeling of intimacy, like amateurish candy made while looking at the recipe book, and I could not resist asking:

"How old is she?"

"Seventeen," Kusano answered. "She's the sister just younger than I."

The more I listened the more I could hear that it was indeed the sound of a piano played by a seventeen-year-old girl, full of dreams and still unaware of her own beauty, whose fingertips still retained traces of childhood. I prayed that her practice would continue forever.

My prayer was answered. In my heart the sound of that piano still continues today, five years later. How many times have I tried to convince myself it is only a hallucination! How many times has my reason ridiculed this delusion! How many times has my weak will laughed at my capacity for self-deception? And for all that the fact remains that the sound of that piano took possession of me, and that for me it was—if the dark connotations can be omitted from the word— veritably a thing of "destiny."

I was remembering the strange impression I had received from this word destiny only a short time before. After the graduation ceremony at higher school, I had gone in an automobile with the old admiral-principal to pay a formal call of gratitude at the Palace. As we drove along, this cheerless old man, with mucous clotted in the corners of his eyes, had criticized my decision not to volunteer as a special cadet but simply await conscription as a common soldier. He had emphasized that, with my physique, I would never be able to endure the rigors of life in the ranks.

"But I've made up my mind."

"You say that because you don't realize what it means. But then the day for volunteering has already passed. So there's nothing to do about it now. It's your *destiny*."

He used the English word, mispronouncing it in the old-fashioned way.

"Huh?" I asked.

"*Destiny*. It's your *destiny*."

He repeated himself in a monotone, using that indifferent, shy tone of voice characteristic of old men who are on their guard against being taken for fussy grandmothers.

During previous visits at Kusano's I must have seen this sister who was playing the piano. But Kusano's family was very strait-laced, not at all like the easygoing Nukada family, and whenever any of Kusano's friends came calling, the three sisters would immediately disappear from sight, leaving only their bashful smiles behind them.

As Kusano's enlistment drew nearer and nearer we visited each other with increasing frequency and were reluctant to part. The experience of hearing that piano had given me a completely wooden manner where that sister was concerned. Hearing it had been like eavesdropping on some secret of hers, and ever since I had somehow become unable to look her directly in the eye or speak to her. When she occasionally brought in the tea, I would keep my eyes lowered and see nothing but her nimble legs and feet moving lightly across the floor. I was completely carried away by the beauty of her legs, perhaps because I had not yet become accustomed to seeing city women wear the bloomer-like trousers of farm women or the slacks that had become the fashion for those perilous times. . . .

And yet it would be a mistake to leave the impression that her legs aroused any sexual excitement in me. As said before, I was completely lacking in any feeling of sexual desire for the opposite sex. This is well proved by the fact that I had never had the slightest wish to see a woman's naked body. For all that, I would begin to imagine seriously that I was in love with a girl, and the spiteful fatigue of which I have spoken would begin to clog my mind; and then next I would find delight in regarding myself as a person ruled by reason and would satisfy my vainglorious desire to appear an adult by likening my frigid and changeable emotions to those of a man who has grown weary from a surfeit of women. Such mental gyrations had become automatic with me, as though I were one of those candy machines that go to work and send a caramel sliding out the moment a coin is inserted.

I had decided I could love a girl without feeling any desire whatsoever. This was probably the most foolhardy undertaking since the beginning of human history. Without being aware of it myself, I was undertaking to be—please forgive my natural inclination toward hyperbole—a Copernicus in the theory of love. In doing so I had obviously arrived unwittingly at nothing more than a belief in the platonic concept of love.

Although probably seeming to contradict what I have said earlier, I believed in this platonic concept honestly, at full face value, purely. In any case was it not purity itself rather than the concept in which I was believing? Was it not purity to which I had sworn allegiance? But more of this later.

If at times I seemed not to believe in platonic love, this too could be blamed on my brain, so apt to prefer the concept of carnal love, which was lacking in my heart, and on that fatigue produced by my artificiality, so apt to accompany any satisfaction of my craze to appear to be an adult. In short, blame it on my unrest.

The last year of the war came and I reached the age of twenty. Early in the year all the students at my university were sent to work at the N airplane factory, near the city of M. Eighty percent of the students became factory hands, while the frail students, who formed the remaining twenty percent, were given some sort of clerical jobs. I fell into the latter category. And yet at the time of my physical examination the year before, I had received the classification of 2(b). Having thus been declared eligible for military service, I had the constant worry that my summons would come tomorrow, if not today.

The airplane factory, located in a desolate area seething with dust, was so huge that it took thirty minutes simply to walk across it from one end to the other, and it hummed with the labor of several thousand workers. I was one of them, bearing the designation of Temporary Employee 953, with Identification No. 4409.

This great factory operated upon a mysterious system of production costs: taking no account of the economic dictum that capital investment should produce a return, it was dedicated to a monstrous nothingness. No wonder then that each morning the workers had to recite a mystic oath. I have never seen such a strange factory. In it all the techniques of modern science and management, together with the exact and rational thinking of many superior brains, were dedicated to a single end—Death. Producing the Zero-model combat plane used by the suicide squadrons, this great factory resembled a secret cult that operated thunderously—groaning, shrieking, roaring. I did not see how such a colossal organization could exist without some religious grandiloquence. And it did in fact possess religious grandeur, even to the way the priestly directors fattened their own stomachs.

From time to time the sirens of the air-raid signals would announce the hour for this perverted religion to celebrate its black mass.

Then the office would begin to stir. There was no radio in the room, so we had no way of knowing what was happening. Someone, speaking in a broad country accent, would say: "Wonder what's up?" About this time a young girl from the reception desk in the superintendent's office would come with some such report as: "Several formations of enemy planes sighted." Before long the strident voices of loud-speakers would order the girl students and the grade-school children to take shelter. Persons in charge of rescue work would walk about distributing red tags bearing the legend "Bleeding stopped: hour____minute____." In case someone was wounded, one of these tags was to be filled in and hung about his neck, showing the time at which a tourniquet had been applied. About ten minutes after the sirens had sounded the loud-speakers would announce: "All employees take shelter."

Grasping files of important papers in their arms, the office workers would hurry to deposit them in the underground vault where essential records were stored. Then they would rush outdoors and join the swarm of laborers running across the square, all wearing air-raid helmets or padded hoods. The crowd would be streaming toward the main gate.

Outside the gate there was a desolate, bare, yellow field. Some seven or eight hundred meters beyond it, numerous shelters had been excavated in a pine grove on a gentle slope. Heading for these shelters, two separate streams of the silent, impatient, blind mob would rush through the dust—rushing toward what at any rate was not Death, no matter if it was only a small cave of easily collapsible red earth, at any rate it was not Death.

I went home on my occasional off days, and there one night at eleven o'clock I received my draft notice. It was a telegram ordering me to report to a certain unit on February the fifteenth.

At my father's suggestion, I had taken my physical examination, not at Tokyo, but at the headquarters of the regiment located near the place where my family maintained its legal residence, in H Prefecture of the Osaka-Kyoto region. My father's theory was that my weak physique would attract more attention in a rural area than in the city, where such weakness was no rarity, and that as a result I would probably not be drafted. As a matter of fact, I had provided the examining officials with cause for an outbreak of laughter when I could not lift—not even as far as my chest—the bale of rice that the farm boys were easily lifting above their heads ten times. And still, in the end I had been classified 2(b).

So now I was summoned—to join a rough rural unit. My mother wept sorrowfully, and even my father seemed no little dejected. As for me, hero though I fancied myself, the sight of the summons aroused no enthusiasm in me; but on the other hand, there was my hope of dying an easy death. All in all, I had the feeling that everything was as it should be.

A cold that I had caught at the factory became much worse as I was going on an interisland steamer to join my unit. By the time I reached the home of close family friends in the village of our legal residence—we had not owned a single bit of land there since my grandfather's bankruptcy—I had such a violent fever that I was unable to stand up. Thanks, however, to the careful nursing I received in that house and especially to the efficacy of the vast quantity of febrifuge I took, I was finally able to make my way through the barracks gate, amidst a spirited send-off given me by the family friends.

My fever, which had only been checked by the medicines, now returned. During the physical examination that preceded final enlistment I had to stand around waiting stark naked, like a wild beast, and I sneezed constantly. The stripling of an army doctor who examined me mistook the wheezing of my bronchial tubes for a chest rattle, and then my haphazard answers concerning my medical history further confirmed him in his error. Hence I was given a blood test, the results of which, influenced by the high fever of my cold, led to a mistaken diagnosis of incipient tuberculosis. I was ordered home the same day as unfit for service.

Once I had put the barracks gate behind me, I broke into a run down the bleak and wintry slope that descended to the villiage. Just as at the airplane factory, my legs carried me running toward something that in any case was not Death—whatever it was, it was not Death. . . .

On the train that night, shrinking from the wind that blew in through a broken window glass, I suffered with fever chills and a headache. Where shall I go now? I asked myself. Thanks to my father's inherent inability to make a final decision about anything, my family still remained unevacuated from our Tokyo house. Shall I go there, to that house where everyone is cowering with suspense? To that city hemming the house in with its dark uneasiness? Into the midst of those crowds where all the people have eyes like cattle and seem always to be wanting to ask each other: "Are you all right? are you all right?" Or to the dormitory of the airplane factory, filled with nothing but the spiritless faces of tubercular university students?

Loosened by the pressure of my back, the wooden planks of the seat against which I leaned were shifting with the vibrations of the train. From time to time I closed my eyes and pictured a scene in which my entire family was annihilated in an air raid that took place while I was visiting them. The mere thought filled me with inexpressible disgust. Nothing gave me such a strange feeling of repugnance as the thought of a connection between everyday life and death. Doesn't even a cat hide itself when death approaches, so that no one may see its dying? Just the thought that I might see the cruel deaths of my family, and that they might see mine, made a retching nausea rise in my chest. The thought of Death's bringing a family to such a pass, of how mother and father and sons and daughters would be overtaken by Death and would share in common the sensation of dying, of the glances they would exchange with one another—to me all this seemed nothing but an obscene travesty on scenes of perfect family happiness and harmony.

What I wanted was to die among strangers, untroubled, beneath a cloudless sky. And yet my desire differed from the sentiments of that ancient Greek who wanted to die under the brilliant sun. What I wanted was some natural, spontaneous suicide. I wanted a death like that of a fox, not yet well versed in cunning, that walks carelessly along a mountain path and is shot by a hunter because of its own stupidity. . . .

If such were the case, wasn't the army ideal for my purpose? Why had I looked so frank as I lied to the army doctor? Why had I said that I'd been having a slight fever for over half a year, that my shoulder was painfully stiff, that I spit blood, that even last night I had been soaked by a night sweat? (This latter happened to be the truth, but small wonder considering the number of aspirin I had taken.) Why when sentenced to return home the same day had I felt the pressure of a smile come pushing so persistently at my lips that I had difficulty in concealing it? Why had I run so when I was through the barracks gate? Hadn't my hopes been blasted? What was the matter that I hadn't hung my head and trudged away with heavy feet?

I realized vividly that my future life would never attain heights of glory sufficient to justify my having escaped death in the army, and hence I could not understand the source of the power which had made me run so rapidly away from the gate of the regiment. Did it mean that I wanted to live after all? And that completely automatic reaction which always made me dash so breathlessly for an air-raid shelter—what was this but a desire to live?

Then suddenly my other voice spoke up within me, telling me that never even once had I truly wanted to die. At these words my sense of shame overflowed the dam behind which it had been confined. It was a painful admission to make, but at that moment I knew I had been lying to myself when I said it was for the sake of death that I wanted to enter the army. At that moment I realized I had been secretly hoping that the army would provide me at last with an opportunity for gratifying those strange sensual desires of mine. And I knew that, far from desiring death, the only thing that had made it at all possible for me to look forward to army life was the firm conviction—arising out of a belief in the primitive art of magic, common to all men —that I alone could never die. . . .

But how disagreeable these thoughts were for me! I much preferred to think of myself instead as a person who had been forsaken even by Death. In the same way that a doctor, performing surgery upon some internal organ, delicately focuses all his faculties upon the operation and still remains impersonal, I delighted in picturing the curious agonies of a person who wanted to die but had been refused by Death. The degree of mental pleasure I thus obtained seemed almost immoral.

The university and the airplane factory had had a difference of opinion, and we had all been withdrawn from the factory at the end of February. The plan was for us to attend lectures again during March and then be mobilized to a different factory in April. But toward the end of February almost a thousand enemy fighter-planes struck, and it became obvious that the lectures scheduled for March would be held in name only.

Thus it came about that we were given a month's vacation at the height of the war. It was like being given a gift of damp fireworks. Nevertheless, I would much rather have received the damp fireworks than some sort of stupidly practical gift that would have been more typical of the university, say a box of soda crackers. It was the sheer extravagance of the thing that pleased me so. The mere fact that it was absolutely useless made it an enormous gift in those days.

A few days after I recovered from my cold, Kusano's mother telephoned. She said that visits to Kusano's regiment near M City were to be allowed for the first time, on March the tenth, and asked if I wouldn't like to go with them to visit Kusano.

I accepted the invitation, and a short time later went to the Kusano house to make arrangements. In those days the hours between dusk and 8 P.M. were regarded as the safest time of day. When I arrived, the family had just finished supper.

As Kusano's father was dead, the family now consisted solely of his mother, grandmother, and three sisters. I was invited to join them around the footwarmer where they were sitting. The mother introduced me to the sister whom I had heard playing the piano that time.

Her name was Sonoko.

Because there was a well-known pianist with the same name, I made a slightly caustic joke concerning the fact that I had previously overheard her practicing the piano. The eighteen-year-old girl blushed in the dim light of the blackout-lamp and said nothing. She was wearing a red-leather jacket.

On the morning of March the ninth I waited for the Kusano family on the platform of a station near their house. The row of shops across the tracks had been condemned by the government to make way for a firebreak, and the work of demolition, already begun, could be seen in detail. The activity tore through the clear air of early spring with fresh, crashing noises. Among the demolished structures there could be seen newly exposed surfaces of naked wood, dazzling to the eye.

The mornings were still cold. For several days not a single air-raid warning had sounded. During that interval the air had become more and more brightly burnished and had been stretched so thin that it now seemed in danger of bursting. The atmosphere was like the tautly tuned string of a samisen, ready to reverberate piercingly at the first pluck. It reminded one of those few moments of silence, rich in emptiness, that are fulfilled in a burst of music. Even the cold sunlight that fell upon the deserted platform was quivering with something like a premonition of music.

Then Sonoko appeared, wearing a blue coat, coming down the opposite stairway with her two sisters. She was holding her smaller sister by the hand, watching her carefully and coming down the steps one at a time. The other sister, then about fourteen or fifteen, seemed impatient at this slow rate of progress, but instead of gradually outstripping the other two she was deliberately coming zigzag down the empty staircase.

Sonoko seemed not to have noticed me yet. From where I stood I could see her clearly. In all my life my heart had never before been so touched by the sight of beauty in a woman. My breast throbbed; I felt purified.

The reader who has followed me this far will probably refuse to believe anything I am saying. He will doubt me because there will seem to be no difference between my artificial and unrequited love of Nukada's sister and the throbbing of the breast of which I am now speaking, because there will seem to be no apparent reason why on this occasion alone I should not have subjected my emotions to that merciless analysis I had used in the former case. If the reader persists in such doubts, then the act of writing has become a useless thing from the beginning: he will think that I say a thing simply because I want to say it so, without any regard for truth, and anything I say will be all right so long as I make my story consistent. Nevertheless, it is a very accurate part of my memory that proclaims a fundamental point of difference between the emotions I had had before this and those that the sight of Sonoko now aroused in me. The difference was that now I had a feeling of remorse.

When she was almost at the bottom of the steps Sonoko noticed me and smiled. Her fresh cheeks were flushed from the cold. Her eyes—their large black pupils and rather heavy lids gave her a slightly sleepy appearance—were glistening as though trying to speak. Then, entrusting the hand of her baby sister to the second sister, she came running down the platform toward me with a graceful motion like the trembling of light.

What I saw come running toward me was not a girl, not that personification of flesh which I had been forcibly picturing to myself since boyhood, but something like the herald of the morning tidings. Had it not been for this fact, I could have met her with my usual fraudulent hopes. But, to my perplexity, my instinct was forced to recognize a different quality in Sonoko alone. This gave me a profound, bashful feeling of being unworthy of Sonoko, and yet it was not a feeling of servile inferiority. Each second while I watched Sonoko approach, I was attacked by unendurable grief. It was a feeling such as I had never had before. Grief seemed to undermine and set tottering the foundations of my existence. Until this moment the feeling with which I had regarded women had been an artificial mixture of childlike curiosity and feigned sexual desire. My heart had never before been swayed, and at first glance, by such a deep and unexplainable grief, a grief moreover that was no part of my masquerade.

I was conscious that the feeling was one of remorse. But had I committed a sin for which I should be remorseful? Although a patent contradiction, is there not a sort of remorse that precedes sin? Was it remorse at the very fact that I existed? Had the sight of her called out to me and awakened this remorse? Or was my feeling possibly nothing but a presentiment of sin? . . .

Sonoko was already standing demurely before me. She had already begun her bow, but finding me lost in thought, she now began it over again, very precisely.

"Have I kept you waiting? Mother and Grand-mother—" She had used the honorific forms in referring to these members of her own family, and now she stopped and blushed, suddenly aware how inappropriate her words were when addressed to someone outside the family circle. "Well, they hadn't finished getting ready yet and will be a little late. So wait a little—" She stopped again, and then corrected herself modestly: "So if you will please wait a little and if they still haven't come, we'll go on ahead to the train station—that is, if you like." Having at last managed to blurt out this long speech in faltering, formal language, she gave a big sigh of relief.

Sonoko had a large build and was tall enough to reach to my forehead. Her body was unusually graceful and well proportioned, and she had beautiful legs. Her round, childlike face, on which she used no make-up, seemed the reflection of an immaculate and unadorned soul. Her lips were slightly chapped and seemed all the redder for it.

We exchanged a few awkward words. Even though I detested myself in the role, I tried with all my might to appear lighthearted and gay, to show myself as a young man abounding in wit.

Any number of elevated trains stopped beside us with shrieking, grating noises, and then departed. The press of passengers getting on and off became heavier and heavier. Each time a train came up we were cut off from the stream of sunlight that was bathing us in its pleasant warmth. And each time a train moved away I would be terrified anew by the gentleness of the sunlight that was let fall again upon my cheeks.

I took it for an ill-omened sign that the richly blessed sunshine should fall upon me thus, that my heart should be thus filled with moments that left nothing to be desired. Surely in a few minutes a sudden air raid or some equally calamitous event would come and kill us where we stood. Surely, I thought, we do not deserve even a little happiness. Or perhaps we had acquired the bad habit of regarding even a little happiness as a big favor, which we would have to repay. This was precisely the feeling I got from being face to face with Sonoko in this way. And Sonoko also seemed to have been overcome with the same feeling.

We waited a long time, but as Sonoko's mother and grandmother did not come, we finally took one of the elevated trains and went on ahead to U Station.

In the bustle at the station we were hailed by a Mr. Ohba who was going to visit his son in the same regiment Kusano was in. This middle-aged banker, who disdained the khaki civilian uniform then in official favor and clung stubbornly to Homburg hat and sack coat, was accompanied by a daughter whom both Sonoko and I knew slightly. Why did I rejoice in the fact that this girl was far from beautiful when compared with Sonoko? What was this feeling? In spite of Sonoko's naïve frolicking, taking place there before my eyes—she was grasping crossed hands with the Ohba girl and making a great show of intimacy—I realized that Sonoko was endowed with the bright magnanimity that is the prerogative of beauty and that this made her appear to be an adult several years older than she actually was.

When we boarded the train it was empty. As though by chance Sonoko and I took seats at a window, facing each other.

Counting the maid who had accompanied them, there were three persons in Mr. Ohba's party. And our party, which had finally been completed, consisted of six. As the two groups made a total of nine, we were one too many to occupy two sets of seats across the aisle from each other.

I had made this quick calculation without even being aware of it. Could Sonoko have been doing the same? At any rate, when we sat down with a plump opposite each other we exchanged mischievous smiles.

In view of the unwieldly number of our combined party, the others tacitly consented when Sonoko and I formed this separate little island for ourselves. As a matter of etiquette Sonoko's grandmother and mother had to sit facing the Ohba father and daughter. Sonoko's younger sister immediately chose a window seat across the aisle, from which she could both see her mother's face and look out the window. The third sister followed her, and their seat became a playground, with the Ohba maid in charge of the two pert girls. Sonoko and I were isolated from all the others by the back of a time-worn seat.

The talkative Mr. Ohba took control of the conversation even before the train left the station. His low-voiced, womanish garrulity left his hearers nothing to do but to agree with him. Even the young-spirited grandmother, who was the talkative representative of the Kusano family, was struck speechless with wonder.

147

Both she and the mother could say nothing but "Yes, yes," and were fully occupied with the task of laughing at important point after important point in Mr. Ohba's monologue. As for the Ohba girl, not a single word passed her lips.

Presently the train began to move. When we were clear of the station the sunlight streamed through the dirty glass of the windows; it fell upon the battered window sill beside which Sonoko and I sat, and spilled over into our laps. Both of us were silent, listening to Mr. Ohba's prattle from the next seat. Now and then a smile flitted across Sonoko's lips; her amusement gradually infected me. Whenever our glances met, Sonoko would assume a sparkling, mischievous, carefree look of listening to the adjacent voice and would avoid my eyes.

". . . And when I die I intend to do so dressed exactly like this. Dying in civilian uniform and leggings, that would be no sort of death, would it? And I won't let my daughter wear slacks either. Isn't it my duty as a father to see that she dies dressed like a woman?"

"Yes, yes."

"By the way, please let me know when you want to evacuate your things from the city. It must be difficult in a household without a man's help. Whatever it is, please let me know."

"You're too kind."

"We've been able to buy a warehouse at T Spa and are

sending the belongings of all our bank clerks there. I can assure you your things would be safe there. Anything you want to send is all right, your piano or anything."

"You're too kind."

"By the way, it's lucky the commander of your son's unit seems to be a good man. I hear my son's commander takes a rake-off from the food brought during visitor's day. Why, it's just the sort of thing you'd expect of those people across the sea. They say the commander always has stomach cramps after visitor's day."

"My, my. . . ."

A smile was again pushing at Sonoko's lips, and she seemed restless. Finally she took a library edition out of the bag she carried. I was a little disappointed, but showed an interest in the title of the book.

"What's that you're reading?" I asked.

She showed me the back of the open book, smiling as she held it up like a fan before her face. The title read *Tale of the Water-Spirit* and was followed, in parentheses, by the original German title, *Undine*.

We could hear someone getting up from the seat behind us. It was Sonoko's mother. I thought she was trying to escape Mr. Ohba's chatter by going to quiet her youngest daughter, who was leaping and jumping on the seat opposite. But as it turned out, she also had a further purpose. She came bringing the noisy girl and her pert older sister to our seat, saying:

"Come now, please let these noisy children join you."

Sonoko's mother was beautiful and graceful. At times the smile that accompanied her gentle way of speaking seemed almost pathetic. As she spoke this time, her smile again impressed me as being rather sad and uneasy. Leaving the two children sitting with us, the mother returned to her seat, while Sonoko and I again snatched a glance at each other. I took a notebook out of my breast pocket and, tearing out a sheet, wrote on it with a pencil:

"Your mother is being careful!"

"What's this?" said Sonoko, cocking her head coyly as I handed her the note. Her hair smelled like a child's. When she had finished reading the words on the piece of paper she blushed to the nape of her neck and cast her eyes down.

"Isn't that right?" I said.

"Oh, I—"

Our eyes met again and we understood each other. I could feel that my cheeks also were bursting into flame.

"Sister, what's that?" The smallest sister reached out her hand.

In a flash Sonoko hid the piece of paper. The other sister was old enough to seem to understand the meaning behind our actions. She became quite angry and pouted. One could tell this from the exaggerated way she began scolding her small sister.

Rather than dampening our spirits, this incident only made it all the easier for Sonoko and me to talk. She spoke about her school, some novels she had been reading, and about her brother. For my part, I soon carried the conversation to general matters, taking the first step in the art of seduction. As we kept talking together so familiarly, ignoring the two sisters, they soon returned to their original seats. They were obviously not very efficient spies, but the mother, again giving her troubled smile, immediately made them come back and sit with us.

By the time we had all gotten settled at an inn in M City, near Kusano's unit, it was already time for bed. One room had been allotted to Mr. Ohba and me.

When we were alone together Mr. Ohba began talking freely, without any attempt to disguise his opposition to further continuation of the war. Such antiwar views were already being whispered whenever people got together, even in the spring of 1945, and I was sick of hearing them. Mr. Ohba babbled on intolerably in his low voice, saying that the big ceramics company in which he had investments was already preparing for peace; that, under the pretext of repairing war damage, they were planning large-scale production of ceramic wares for household use; and that it seemed we were making peace offers through the Soviet Union.

As for me, there was something I much more wanted

to think about by myself. Finally the light was turned off and Mr. Ohba's face, which had looked strangely swollen without his glasses, disappeared into the shadows. His innocent sighs slowly pervaded all the bedding two or three times and then his deep breathing showed he was asleep. Feeling the fresh cover, which had been wrapped about the pillow, scratching against my flushed cheeks, I became lost in thought.

Added to the gloomy irritation that always threatened me when I was alone, the grief that had so shaken the foundations of my existence this morning when I had seen Sonoko was now revived still more poignantly within my heart. It proclaimed that every word I had spoken and every act I had performed that day had been false: having discovered that it was less painful to decide a thing was false in its entirety than to torture myself with doubts as to which part might be true and which false, I had already become gradually familiar with this way of deliberately unmasking my falseness to myself. And even as I lay thinking, my tenacious uneasiness concerning what I called the basic condition of being a human being, concerning what I called the positive human psychology, did nothing but lead me around in endless circles of introspection.

How would I feel if I were another boy? How would I feel if I were a normal person? These questions obsessed me. They tortured me, instantly and utterly destroying even the one splinter of happiness I had thought I possessed for sure.

My "act" has ended by becoming an integral part of my nature, I told myself. It's no longer an act. My knowledge that I am masquerading as a normal person has even corroded whatever of normality I originally possessed, ending by making me tell myself over and over again that it too was nothing but a pretense at normality. To say it another way, I'm becoming the sort of person who can't believe in anything except the counterfeit. But if this is true, then my feeling of wanting to regard Sonoko's attraction for me as sheer counterfeit might be nothing but a mask to hide my true desire of believing myself genuinely in love with her. So maybe I am becoming the sort of person who is incapable of acting contrary to his true nature, and maybe I do really love her. . . .

With such thoughts as these weaving circles inside my head I was finally almost on the point of going to sleep when suddenly, borne on the night air, there came that wailing sound which was always ominous but still somehow fascinating.

"Isn't that the alarm?" the banker said immediately. I was startled by the lightness of his sleep.

"I wonder," I answered vaguely.

The sirens continued sounding faintly for a long time.

As the hours for visiting the regiment began early in the morning, we all arose at six o'clock.

Sonoko was in the washroom when I went in. After exchanging good mornings with her, I said:

"The sirens blew last night, didn't they?"

"No," she replied with a straight face.

When we returned to our adjoining rooms, where the connecting door had been thrown open, her answer to my question provided her sisters with good material for teasing her:

"Sister was the only one who didn't hear the sirens. My, how funny!" the smaller sister said, following the other's lead.

"Me, I woke up right away, and heard Sister's loud snoring."

"That's right. I heard her too. She was snoring so loud that I could hardly hear the sirens."

"That's what you say, but you can't prove it." Because I was present, Sonoko was blushing deeply and putting up a bold front. "If you tell such lies, you'll be sorry later."

I had only one sister. Ever since childhood I had longed for a lively family with many sisters. To my ears this half-joking, noisy quarrel among the sisters sounded as a most splendid and genuine reflection of worldly happiness. It also reawakened my anguish.

The sole subject of conversation during breakfast was last night's air-raid warning, which was the first since early March. Since there had been only the warning signal and the signal of an actual attack had not sounded after all, everyone calmed down and concluded that nothing much could have happened. As for me, it made no difference either way. I told myself that even if my house had burned to the ground while I was away, even if my mother, father, brother, and sister had all been killed, that would be quite all right with me.

At the time this did not seem a particularly cold-blooded thought. In those days our powers of imagination had been made the poorer by the fact that the most fantastic event which we could imagine might actually happen any moment as a matter of course. It was far easier to imagine the annihilation of one's entire family than to picture things that now belonged to a distant, impossible past, say an array of bottles of imported liquors in a Ginza shopwindow, or the sight of neon signs flickering in the night sky over the Ginza. As a result our imagination confined itself to easier paths. Imagination like this, which follows the path of least resistance, has no connection with coldness of heart, no matter how cruel it may appear. It is nothing but a product of a lazy, tepid mind.

In contrast to the tragic role in which I had cast myself during the night, when we left the inn the next morning I instantly wanted to play the lighthearted cavalier and carry Sonoko's bag. This too was with the deliberate intention of producing an effect within sight of everyone. If I insist on carrying her bag for her, I told myself, she is sure to protest, simply out of her natural feeling of reserve toward me; but her mother and grandmother will think we must already be on affectionate terms and will interpret her hesitation as fear of what they might be thinking; and as a result she herself will be tricked in turn into a clear awareness of a feeling of sufficient intimacy with me to make her fear her mother and grandmother.

My little ruse was successful. She remained by my side, as though the entrusting of her bag to my hands had given her a reasonable excuse for doing so. Even though the Ohba girl was a friend of the same age, Sonoko took no notice of her and talked only with me. I glanced at Sonoko from time to time with a strange feeling. Her voice, so sweet and pure that it made me feel somehow sad, was blown to pieces by the dust-laden wind of early spring, which came blowing directly in our faces.

I raised and lowered my shoulder, testing the weight of her bag. Its weight scarcely justified the feeling that was growing deeply within my heart, a feeling like the guilty conscience of a fugitive from justice.

As we reached the outskirts of town Sonoko's grandmother began complaining of the distance. The banker retraced his steps to the station, where he must have used some clever trick in order to rent the two cars—so scarce in those days—with which he presently returned.

"Hey! it's been a long time."

I shook Kusano's hand and was as startled as if I had grasped the shell of a spiny lobster.

"Your hand—what's the matter with it?"

Kusano laughed. "You're surprised, aren't you?"

His body had already acquired that somehow dispirited pitifulness which is the special characteristic of a new recruit. He stretched his hands out for me to see, holding them side by side. They were badly chapped, with hardened dirt and oil ground into their cracks and scratches and chilblains until they did indeed resemble the shell of a lobster. They were also damp and cold.

His hands frightened me in the same way that reality did. I felt an instinctive terror of those hands. What I actually feared was something within me that these relentless hands had revealed, something for which they accused and condemned me. It was a fear that I could hide nothing from them, that all deception would be unavailing before them. Instantly Sonoko took on a new meaning for me—she was my sole armor, the sole coat of mail for my frail conscience in its struggle against these hands. Right or wrong, by fair means or foul, I told myself, you simply *must* love her. This feeling became, as it were, a moral obligation for me, lying even heavier in the bottom of my heart than did my sense of sin.

Knowing nothing of all this, Kusano said innocently:

"You don't need a washrag for a bath when you've got hands like these to rub with."

A tiny sigh escaped from his mother's lips. In my

position I could not help feeling like a shameless, uninvited guest. Sonoko happened to glance up at me. I hung my head. Absurd as it was, I had a feeling as though I must ask her forgiveness for something.

"Let's go outside," said Kusano, pushing roughly at the backs of his grandmother and mother in his embarrassment.

Each family group was seated in a circle on the dead turf of the bleak barracks courtyard, treating its cadet to a feast. I regret to say that no matter how I looked I could find no beauty in the scene.

Soon we too had formed a circle of our own, with Kusano sitting cross-legged in the middle of it. He was cramming some Western-style candies into his mouth and could only roll his eyes when he wanted to call my attention to the sky in the direction of Tokyo. From the hilly region where we were I could look across sear fields to the basin in which M City lay extended. And beyond it I could look between a gap formed by the meeting of two low mountain ranges to what Kusano said was the sky over Tokyo. The chilly clouds of early spring were spreading their shadows over that distant region.

"Last night the sky was bright red there. It was something awful. There's no telling whether your house is still standing or not. There's never been an air raid before that made all the sky there turn so red. . . ."

No one spoke. Kusano went on chattering importantly, complaining that unless his grandmother and mother evacuated the family to the country as soon as possible he'd never be able to get a full night's sleep.

"I agree with you," the grandmother said spiritedly. "We'll evacuate right away. I promise you." From her obi she extracted a small notebook and a silver pencil no larger than a toothpick and began writing something painstakingly.

On the return journey the train was filled with gloom. Even Mr. Ohba, whom we had met by appointment at the station, seemed a different person and held his tongue. Everyone had the air of having been taken prisoner by the feeling commonly called "love of one's own flesh and blood"; it was as though the emotions one normally keeps hidden within had been turned inside out and were smarting painfully with rawness. They had met their sons, brothers, grandsons, with a showing of naked hearts—it was all they had to show —and now, on top of this, they probably realized it had all been nothing but a futile outpouring of blood before each other. As for me, I was still pursued by the vision of those pitiful hands. It was almost dusk, almost time for lights to be turned on, when our train reached the station on the outskirts of Tokyo where we were to transfer to the elevated.

Here for the first time we were brought face to face with positive evidence of the damage that had been done in the air raid the night before. The passageway over the tracks was filled with victims of the raid. They were wrapped up in blankets until one could see nothing but their eyes or, better said, nothing but their eyeballs, for they were eyes that saw nothing and thought nothing. There was a mother who seemed to intend to rock the child in her lap eternally, never varying by so much as a hairsbreadth the length of the arc through which she swayed her body, back and forth, back and forth. A girl was sleeping, leaning against a piece of wicker luggage, still wearing scorched artificial flowers in her hair.

As we went along the passageway we did not receive even so much as a reproachful glance. We were ignored. Our very existence was obliterated by the fact that we had not shared in their misery; for them, we were nothing more than shadows.

In spite of this scene something caught fire within me. I was emboldened and strengthened by the parade of misery passing before my eyes. I was experiencing the same excitement that a revolution causes. In the fire these miserable ones had witnessed the total destruction of every evidence that they existed as human beings. Before their eyes they had seen human relationships, loves and hatreds, reason, property, all go up in flame. And at the time it had not been the flames against which they fought, but against human relationships, against loves and hatreds, against reason, against property. At the time, like the crew of a wrecked ship, they had found themselves in a situation where it was permissible to kill one person in order that another might live. A man who died trying to rescue his sweetheart was killed, not by the flames, but by his sweetheart; and it was none other than the child who murdered its own mother when she was trying to save it. The condition they had faced and fought against there—that of a life for a life—had probably been the most universal and elemental that mankind ever encounters.

In their faces I saw traces of that exhaustion which comes from witnessing a spectacular drama. Some hot feeling of confidence poured into me. Though it was only for a few seconds, I felt that all my doubts concerning the fundamental requirement of manhood had been totally swept away. My breast was filled with a desire to shout. Perhaps if I had been a little richer in the power of self-understanding, if I had been blessed with a little more wisdom, I could have gone on to a close examination of that requirement and could finally have understood the real meaning of myself as a human being. Instead, comically enough, the warmth of a kind of fantasy made me put my arm around Sonoko's waist for the first time. Perhaps this action and the brotherly, protective spirit that prompted it had already shown me that what is called love had no meaning for me. If so, it was a sudden insight into truth, which was forgotten just as quickly as it came. . . .

With my arm still around her waist, we walked in front of the others and passed hurriedly through the gloomy passageway. Sonoko said not a word.

We got on the elevated train, and its lights seemed strangely bright. I could see Sonoko gazing at me. Her eyes, though still black and soft, seemed somehow urgently pleading.

When we transferred to the metropolitan loop line, about ninety percent of the passengers were air-raid victims. Now there was an even more noticeable smell of fire. They were loud and boastful as they related to each other the dangers they had undergone. In the true sense of the word, this was a rebellious mob: it was a mob that harbored a radiant discontent, an overflowing, triumphant, high-spirited dissatisfaction.

Reaching S Station, where I was to part from the others, I returned Sonoko's bag to her and got off. As I walked along the pitch-dark streets to my house I was reminded over and over again that my hands were no longer carrying her bag. At last I recognized the important role which that bag had played in our relationship. It had served as a tiny drudgery, and for me the weight of some sort of drudgery was always needed to keep my conscience from raising its head too high.

When I arrived home the family greeted me as though nothing had happened. After all, Tokyo covers a vast area and even such an air raid as that of the night before could not affect it all.

A few days later I visited the Kusano house, taking some books I had promised to lend Sonoko. There will be no need to give their titles when I say they were just the sort of novels that a young man of twenty should choose for a girl of eighteen. I experienced an unusual delight in doing the conventional thing. Sonoko happened to be out, but was expected back soon. I waited for her in the parlor.

While I was waiting, the sky of early spring became as cloudy as lye; it began to rain. Sonoko had apparently been caught in the rain on her way home, for when she came into the gloomy parlor drops of water still glistened here and there in her hair. Shrugging her shoulders, she sat down in the shadows at one end of the deep sofa. Again a smile spread across her lips. She was wearing a crimson jacket, from which the roundness of her breasts seem to loom up in the thin darkness.

How timidly we talked, with what a paucity of words! This was the first opportunity we had ever had to be alone together. It was obvious that the carefree way we had talked to each other on that brief train journey had been due largely to the presence of the chatterbox behind us and of the two sisters. Today there remained not a vestige of that boldness which, only a few days before, had led me to hand her a one-line love letter written on a scrap of paper.

Even more than before I was overcome with a feeling of humbleness. I was a person who could not help becoming serious whenever I let my guard down, but I was not afraid to do so before her. Had I forgotten my act? Had I forgotten that I was determined to fall utterly in love like any other person? However that may be, I had not the slightest feeling of being in love with this refreshing girl. And yet I felt at ease with her.

The shower stopped and the setting sun shone into the room. Sonoko's eyes and lips gleamed. Her beauty depressed me, making me remember my own feeling of helplessness. This painful feeling made Sonoko seem all the more ephemeral.

"As for us," I blurted out, "who knows how long we'll live? Suppose there were an air raid at this minute. Probably one of the bombs would fall directly on us."

"Wouldn't that be wonderful!" She was serious. She had been toying with the pleats of her Scotch-plaid skirt, folding them back and forth, but as she said this she lifted her face and the light caught a sparkle of faint down on her cheeks. "Oh—if only a plane would come silently and make a direct hit on us while we're here like this—Don't you think so?" She did not realize that she was making a confession of love.

"H'm. . . . Yes, that'd be fine," I replied in a conversational tone. Sonoko could not possibly have realized how deeply my answer was rooted in my secret desire. When I think back over it now, this dialogue strikes me as highly humorous. It was a conversation that, in peacetime, could have taken place only between two persons who were deeply in love.

164

"I'm really fed up with being separated by death and lifelong partings," I said, adopting a cynical tone to cover my embarrassment. "Don't you sometimes feel that, in times like these, to separate is normal and to meet is the miracle . . . that, when you think of it, even our being able to meet and talk together like this for a time is probably quite a miraculous thing? . . ."

"Yes, I also . . ." She started speaking with some hesitation. Then she went on with an earnest but agreeable serenity. "But here when I was thinking we'd just begun meeting already we're to be separated. Grandmother is in a hurry to leave. As soon as we came home the other day, she sent a telegram to my aunt at N Village in N Prefecture, asking her to find a house for us. This morning my aunt called by long distance and said there're no houses to be had, no matter how you search. So she asked us to come and stay at her house. She said she'd be happy to have us because we'd make her house livelier. Grandmother made her mind up on the spot and said we'd come within two or three days."

I could not make a casual reply. The pain I felt in my heart was so piercing that it surprised even me. The feeling of ease I felt with Sonoko had given me an illusion, a belief that all our days would be spent together and that everything would remain just as it was now. In a deeper sense it was a twofold illusion: the words with which she passed the sentence of separation upon us proclaimed the meaninglessness of our present meeting and revealed that my present feeling was only a passing happiness, and at the same time as they destroyed the childish illusion of believing this would last forever, they also opened my eyes to the fact that, even if there were no parting, no relationship between a boy and girl could ever remain just as it was.

It was a painful awakening. Why were things wrong just as they were? The questions which I had asked myself numberless times since boyhood rose again to my lips. Why are we all burdened with the duty to destroy everything, change everything, entrust everything to impermanency? Is it this unpleasant duty that the world calls life? Or am I the only one for whom it is a duty? At least there was no doubt that I was alone in regarding the duty as a heavy burden.

At last I spoke:

"So, you're leaving. . . . But of course even if you were here, I myself would have to be going away before long. . . ."

"Where're you going?"

"They've decided to send us to live and work at some factory again beginning this month or in April."

"But a factory—that'll be dangerous, with the air raids and all."

"Yes, it'll be dangerous," I answered despairfully.

I took my leave as quickly as possible. . . .

All the following day I was in a carefree mood inspired by the thought of having already been relieved of the obligation to love her. I was cheerful, singing in a loud voice, kicking aside the disgusting Compendium of Laws.

This curiously sanguine state of mind lasted the entire day. That night I fell asleep like a child. Then suddenly I was awakened by the sound of sirens blowing far and wide in the middle of the night. All the household went to the air-raid shelter grouchily, but no planes appeared and soon the all-clear siren sounded. Having dozed off in the shelter, I was the last to emerge above ground, my steel helmet and canteen dangling from my shoulder.

The winter of 1945 had been a persistent one. Although spring had already arrived, coming with the stealthy footsteps of a leopard, winter still stood like a cage about it, blocking its way with gray stubbornness. Ice still glittered under the starlight.

Through the foliage of an evergreen tree my wakeful eyes picked out several stars, which looked warmly blurred. The sharp night air mingled with my breathing. Suddenly I was overwhelmed by the idea that I was in love with Sonoko and that a world in which Sonoko and I both did not live was not worth a penny to me. Something inside told me that if I could forget her I'd better do so. And immediately, as though it had been lying in wait, that grief which undermined the foundations of my existence flooded over me again, just as it had that day when I saw Sonoko coming down the steps onto the platform.

The grief was unendurable. I stamped the ground. Nevertheless I held out one more day.

Then I could stand it no longer and went to see her. The packers were at work just outside the front door. There on the gravel they were tying straw ropes around something like an oblong chest, wrapped in straw matting. The sight filled me with uneasiness.

It was the grandmother who came to meet me in the entryway. Behind her I could see piles of goods that had already been packed and were waiting to be carried out. The hallway was full of waste straw. Noticing the grandmother's slightly embarrassed expression, I decided to leave at once without seeing Sonoko.

"Please give these books to Miss Sonoko." Like an errand boy from a book shop I again held out several sugary novels.

"Thank you so much for all you've done," the grandmother said, making no move to call Sonoko. "We've decided to leave for N Village tomorrow evening. Everything has worked out without a bit of trouble and so we can leave earlier than we'd planned. Mr. T has rented this house as a dormitory for his employees. Truly it is sad to say good-bye. All the children were so happy knowing you, so please come to visit us at N Village too. We'll send you word when we're settled, so be sure and come to see us."

It was pleasant to hear the grandmother's precise and sociable way of speaking. But, just like her too-well-shaped false teeth, her words were nothing but a perfect alignment of some sort of inorganic matter.

"I hope all of you stay well" was all I could say. I could not bring myself to speak Sonoko's name.

Then, as though summoned by my hesitation, Sonoko appeared in the hall at the foot of the stairs. She was carrying a large cardboard hatbox in one hand and several books in the other. Her hair was ablaze in the light that entered from an overhead window. Seeing me, she cried out, startling her grandmother:

"Please wait a minute."

She raced back upstairs, her footsteps sounding boisterously. I was elated by the sight of the grandmother's astonishment, as it made me realize how much Sonoko must love me. The old lady apologized, saying the entire house was in a mess and there was no room in which to receive me. Then she disappeared busily into the interior.

Soon Sonoko came running back down. Her face was very red. She put on her shoes without saying a word, while I stood petrified in one corner of the entryway. Then she stood up and said she would accompany me as far as the station. There was a strength in the commandingly high pitch of her voice that moved me. Although I continued gazing at her and turning my uniform cap round and round in my hands with a naïve gesture, within my heart there was a feeling as though everything had suddenly become motionless. Keeping close together, we went out the door and walked silently along the gravel path to the gate.

Suddenly Sonoko stopped to retie a shoelace. She seemed to be taking a curiously long time about it, so I walked on to the gate and waited, looking out at the street. I did not yet realize that she had wanted me to walk on a little ahead of her and had employed this charming technique of an eighteen-year-old girl for just that purpose.

Suddenly, from behind me, her hand plucked at the sleeve of my uniform. The shock I felt was like being hit by an automobile while walking along absent-mindedly.

"... Please ... this ..."

The corner of a stiff foreign-style envelope touched my palm. I closed my hand upon it so quickly that I all but crushed it, just as one might strangle a baby bird. Somehow I could not believe my senses as I felt the weight of the envelope in my hand. But there it was, an envelope of the kind favored by schoolgirls, held tightly in my own hand; I blinked at it as though it were something a person ought not to look at.

"Not now—read it after you're home," she whispered in a voice that was small and choking, as though she had been tickled.

"Where shall I send a reply?" I asked.

"I wrote it—it's inside—the address in N Village. Write me there."

It is an amusing thing, but suddenly, parting became a delight for me. It was like the pleasure of that moment in a game of hide-and-seek when the person who is "it" counts and everyone runs to hide, each in the direction that pleases him. I had an odd ability to enjoy everything in this way. Because of this perverse talent my cowardice was often mistaken, even in my own eyes, for courage.

We parted at the ticket gate of the station, not even shaking hands.

I was in ecstasy over having received the first love letter of my life. I could not wait until I was home to read it, and I opened the envelope there in the elevated car, heedless of all eyes. As I did so the contents all but spilled out. There were several silhouette-cards and a sheaf of those imported colored postcards that seem to be the delight of mission-school students. Among them was a doublefold of blue notepaper, decorated with a Disney cartoon of Red Riding Hood and the Wolf. Under the cartoon her note was written in neat characters that smacked of painstaking penmanship:

"I was truly overwhelmed with gratitude for your kindness in lending me the books. Thanks to you, I have been able to read them with very profound interest. I pray with all my heart that you will be well even during the air raids. When I have reached my destination and settled down I shall write you again. My address there is given below. The enclosures are trifling things, but please accept them as tokens of my gratitude." . . .

What a magnificent love letter! It pierced the bubble of my ecstasy. I became deathly pale and burst out laughing. Who would answer such a letter as this, I asked myself. It would be as stupid as acknowledging a printed letter of thanks.

However, from the beginning I had felt a desire to send a reply, and now, during the thirty or forty minutes that yet remained before arriving home, this desire gradually arose to the defense of the first "state of ecstasy" I had ever had. The training she receives at home, I immediately told myself, is scarcely the kind to make her proficient in the writing of love letters. Because it's only natural that her hand should be cramped by all sorts of doubts and hestitations and shyness when writing her first letter to a boy. Because every movement she made this afternoon revealed a truer story than any word in this empty letter.

Arriving home, I was suddenly seized with anger from a different quarter. Again I snarled at the Compendium of Laws and hurled it against the wall of my room. What a sluggard you are, I reproached myself. When you're face to face with a girl of eighteen you wait covetously for her to fall in love with you. Why wasn't it you who took the offensive? I know you hesitate because of that queer uneasiness of yours, which comes from you don't know where. But if that's the case, why did you ever visit her again? Think back! —when you were about fourteen you were a boy like other boys. And even at sixteen you were keeping up with them on the whole. But how about now, when you're twenty? That friend of yours said you'd die when you were nineteen, but his prediction didn't come true, and then you even lost your desire to die on a battlefield. Now that you're twenty you're at your wit's end with calf love for an eighteen-year-old girl who knows absolutely nothing. Phew! what splendid progress! At the age of twenty you're planning to exchange love letters for the first time— haven't you maybe made a mistake in counting your age? And isn't it also true that you've never even yet kissed a girl? What a sad specimen you are!

Then again a different voice mocked me, secret and persistent. This voice was filled with an almost feverish honesty, a human feeling I had never experienced before. It bombarded me with questions in quick succession: Is it love you feel? If so, all right. But do you have a desire for women? Aren't you deceiving yourself when you say that it's toward her alone that you have never had a "lustful desire"? Aren't you trying to hide from yourself the fact that actually you've never had a "lustful desire" for any woman? What right on earth do you have to use the word "lustful"? Have you ever had the slightest desire to see a woman naked? Have you ever once imagined Sonoko naked? You, with your special knack at drawing analogies—surely you must have guessed a thing as obvious as the fact that a boy your age is never able to look at a young girl without imagining how she'd look naked. Ask yourself honestly why I tell you this. Go ahead, use your analogies—you'll have to change only one small detail to understand how other boys feel. Just last night didn't you indulge in your little habit before you went to sleep? Call it something like praying if you want. Say it's just a tiny pagan ceremony that everybody performs—all right. Even a substitute is not unpleasant once you get used to it, especially when you find it to be such an instantly effective sleeping draught. But remember that it wasn't a picture of Sonoko that arose in your mind last night. Whatever it was, your fantasy was strange and unnatural enough to amaze even me who have become so accustomed to watching by your side.

During the day you walk down the street and see no one but the sailors and soldiers. They're the youths for you—just the age you like, well tanned by the sun, unsophisticated lips, and not a trace of the intellectual about them. Whenever you see one you immediately take his measure with your eye. Apparently you intend to become something like a tailor when you graduate from law school—is that it? You have a great fondness for the lithe body of a simple young man of around twenty, a body like that of a lion cub, don't you? How many such young men didn't you mentally strip of their clothes yesterday? Your imagination is like one of those kits used for collecting plant specimens. Into it you gather the naked bodies of all these ephebes seen during the day, and then when you're home and in bed you select from your collection the ritual sacrifice for your pagan ceremony, singling out one who has caught your particular fancy. What follows then is thoroughly disgusting:

You lead your victim to a curious hexagonal pillar, hiding a rope behind you. Then you bind his naked body to the pillar with the rope, stretching his arms above his head. You insist that he put up plenty of resistance and scream loudly. You give the victim an elaborate description of his approaching death, and all the while a strange, innocent smile plays about your lips. Taking a sharp knife from your pocket, you press close to him and tickle the skin of his straining chest with the point of the knife, lightly and caressingly. He gives a despairing cry, twisting his body in an effort to escape the knife; his breath roars with terrified panting; his legs tremble and his knees knock together with a clatter. Slowly the knife is driven into the side of his chest. (That's the outrageous thing you did!) The victim arches his body, giving a lonely, piteous shriek, and there is a spasm in the muscles around the wound. The knife has been buried in the rippling flesh as calmly as though being inserted in a scabbard. A fountain of blood bubbles up, pours out, and goes flowing down toward his smooth thighs.

The pleasure you experience at this moment is a genuine human feeling. I say so because at this precise moment you possess the normality that is your obsession. Whatever the form of your fantasy, you are sexually excited to the very depths of your physical being, and such excitement is entirely normal, differing not a jot from that of other men. Your mind quivers under the rush of primitive, mysterious excitement. The deep joy of a savage is reborn in your breast. Your eyes shine, the blood blazes up throughout your body, and you overflow with that manifestation of life worshiped by savage tribes. Even after ejaculation a fevered, savage chant of exultation remains in your body; you are not attacked by that sadness which follows intercourse with a woman. You glitter with debauched loneliness. For a little while you are floating in the memory of a huge, ancient river. Perhaps by some chance the memory of the deepest emotion in the life force of your savage ancestors has taken utter possession of your sexual functions and pleasures. But you're too busy with your pretending to notice, aren't you? I cannot understand why you, who can thus sometimes feel the deep pleasure of human existence, find it necessary to utter such drivel about love and soul.

I tell you what—how about this idea? What if you were to present your magnum opus of a quaint doctoral thesis in the presence of Sonoko? It's a profound dissertation entitled "Concerning the Functional Relationships between an Ephebe's Torso-Curves and Rate of Blood Flow." In short, the torso you select for your daydream is one that is smooth and supple and solid, above all a young torso on which the blood will trace the most subtle curves as it flows from the knife wound. Isn't that right? Don't you select the torso that will produce the most beautiful and natural patterns in the flowing blood, patterns like those made by a meandering stream which flows across a plain, or like the grain in a cross section of an ancient tree? Can you deny this? ...

I could not deny it.

And yet my powers of self-analysis were constructed in a way that defied definition, like one of those hoops made by giving a single twist to a strip of paper and then pasting the ends together. What appeared to be the inside was the outside, and what appeared the outside was the inside. Although in later years my self-analysis traversed the rim of the hoop more slowly, when I was twenty it was doing nothing but spin blindfolded through the orbit of my emotions, and lashed on by the excitement attending the war's final disastrous stages, the speed of the revolutions had become enough to make me all but completely lose my sense of balance. There was no time for a careful consideration of causes and effects, no time for either contradictions or correlations.

So the contradictions spun on through the orbit just as they were, rubbing together with a speed that no eye could comprehend.

After almost an hour of this, the only thought that remained in my mind was that of composing some clever answer to Sonoko's letter. . . .

Meanwhile the cherry trees had blossomed. But no one seemed to have time for flower-viewing; the students from my school were probably the only people in Tokyo who had the opportunity of seeing the cherry blossoms. On my way home from the university, either alone or with two or three friends, I often strolled beneath the cherry trees around S Pond.

The blossoms seemed unusually lovely this year. There were none of the scarlet-and-white-striped curtains that are set up among the blossoming trees so invariably that one has come to think of them as the attire of cherry blossoms; there were no bustling tea-stalls, no holiday crowds of flower-viewers, no one hawking balloons and toy windmills; instead there were only the cherry trees blossoming undisturbed among the evergreens, making one feel as though he were seeing the naked bodies of the blossoms. Nature's free bounty and useless extravagance had never appeared so fantastically beautiful as it did this spring. I had an uncomfortable suspicion that Nature had come to reconquer the earth for herself. Certainly there was something unusual about this spring's brilliance. The yellow of the rape blossoms, the green of the young grass, the fresh-looking black trunks of the cherry trees, the canopy of heavy blossoms that bent the branches low—all these were reflected in my eyes as vivid colors tinged with malevolence. It seemed to be a conflagration of colors.

One day several of us walked along on the grass between the rows of cherry trees and the banks of the pond, arguing some nonsensical legal theory as we went. At the time I was fond of the irony of Professor Y's lectures on international law. In the very midst of the air raids, there the professor was, broad-mindedly continuing his seemingly endless lectures about the League of Nations. I felt as though I were listening to lectures on mahjong or chess. Peace! peace!—I could not believe that this bell-like sound which was perpetually tolling in the distance was anything more than a ringing in my ears.

"But isn't it a question of the absolute nature of real-property claims?" suggested A, continuing our discussion. Although this countrified student seemed to be a strapping fellow with a healthy complexion, an advanced case of lung seepage had saved him from being drafted.

"Let's cut out such foolish talk," broke in B. He was a pale student and, as could be told at a glance, was suffering from tuberculosis.

"In the air enemy planes, on the ground law—

humph!" I laughed scornfully. "Is this what you mean by glory in the heavens and peace on earth?"

I was the only one who did not have genuine lung trouble. I was pretending instead that I had a bad heart. In those days one had to have either medals or illness.

Suddenly we were brought to a halt by the sound of someone walking nearby in the grass under the cherry trees. That person also seemed to have been startled by our approach. It was a young man wearing soiled work clothes and wooden clogs. One could tell he was young only from the color of the close-cropped hair that could be seen beneath his field cap; his muddy complexion, his sparse beard, his oil-smeared hands and feet, and his grimy neck, all indicated a wretched tiredness unsuitable to his years.

Obliquely behind the boy there stood a girl, who stared at the ground and seemed to be sulking. Her hair was slicked back in a hasty, efficient fashion, and she was wearing the ubiquitous khaki blouse. The sole thing about the couple which appeared wonderfully fresh and clean and new was the pair of bloomer-like work pants the girl was wearing.

One could easily guess that they were conscript workers in the same factory and had m t here for a rendezvous, playing truant from the factc y and coming for a day of flower-viewing. Hearing us, they had probably been alarmed by the thought that we might be gendarmes.

They glanced at us unpleasantly as they passed by. After that we did not feel like talking much.

Before the cherry blossoms were gone the Law Department suspended lectures again and we were sent on student mobilization to a naval arsenal a few miles from S Bay. At the same time my mother, brother, and sister evacuated to my maternal grandfather's house, on a small farm in the suburbs. Our houseboy, a middle-school student who, though small in size, acted much older than his years, remained in our Tokyo house to take care of my father. On riceless days the houseboy brayed boiled soybeans in a mortar and made a gruel, which looked like vomit, for my father and himself. He also stealthily consumed our small stock of pickled vegetables when my father was not at home.

Life at the naval arsenal was easygoing. I was assigned some part-time work in the library, and the rest of the time I was on a digging detail with a group of young Formosan laborers, digging a large lateral tunnel for the evacuation of the parts-manufacturing plant. Those little devils of twelve or thirteen were the only companions I had. They gave me lessons in Formosan and in exchange I told them fairy tales. They were confident that their Formosan gods would save them from the air raids and return them one day unharmed to their native land. Their appetites reached immoral proportions. One shrewd boy among them spirited away some rice and vegetables from under the eyes of the kitchen guard, and they made it into fried rice by cooking it in a copious amount of machine oil. I declined this feast, which seemed to have the flavor of gears.

Within less than a month my correspondence with Sonoko was on the way to becoming a very special one. In my letters I behaved with unreserved boldness. One morning I returned to my desk in the arsenal after an all-clear siren had sounded and found a letter from Sonoko awaiting me. My hands shook as I read it and my body felt as though I were slightly intoxicated. There was one line in her letter which I repeated over and over under my breath:

". . . I am longing for you. . . ."

Absence had emboldened me. Distance had given me claim to "normality." I had, so to speak, accepted "normality" as a temporary employee in the corporation of my body. A person who is separated from one by time and space takes on an abstract quality. Perhaps this was the reason why the blind devotion I felt for Sonoko and my ever-present unnatural desires of the flesh had now been fused within me into a single homogenous mass and had pinned me immobile to each succeeding instant of time as a human being without any self-contradictions.

I was free. Everyday life had become a thing of unspeakable happiness. There was a rumor that the enemy would probably make a landing soon in S Bay and that the region in which the arsenal stood would be overwhelmed. And again, even more than before, I found myself deeply immersed in a desire for death. It was in death that I had discovered my real "life's aim."

One Saturday in mid-April I received permission to take the first leave I had been granted in a long time. I went first to the house in Tokyo, planning to get some books from my bookcase for reading at the arsenal and then go on at once to spend the night at my grandfather's place in the suburbs, where my mother and the others were living. But on the way, while the train was starting and stopping in obedience to the air-raid signals, I had a sudden chill. I felt violently dizzy and a hot languor spread through my body. From frequent experience I recognized the symptoms as tonsilitis. As soon as I reached the Tokyo house I had the houseboy spread the covers and went right to bed.

Before long the animated sound of a woman's voice rose from downstairs and grated against my fevered forehead. I heard someone mount the stairs and come tripping down the corridor. Opening my eyes slightly, I saw the skirt of a large-patterned kimono.

". . . What's this? What a lazy person you are!"

"Oh," I said, "hello, Chako."

"What do you mean saying just 'Oh hello' when we haven't met for almost five years?"

She was the daughter of a family distantly related to us. Her name of Chieko had been twisted into Chako, and this was what we all called her. She was five years my senior. The last time I had seen her had been at her wedding. But last year her husband had died at the front, and people had begun gossiping about her, saying she was becoming strangely lighthearted. Now I saw how true the gossip was, and in the face of such animation I could not offer the usual condolences. I kept a shocked silence, thinking to myself that she'd have done better to have left off the large white artificial flowers she had in her hair.

"Today I came to see Tatchan on business," she said, calling my father by the familiar form of his name Tatsuo. "I came to ask about the evacuation of our things. Because the other day Papa and Tatchan met some place and he said he could recommend a good place for us to send the things to."

"The old man said he would be a little late coming home today. But never mind—" Seeing her too-crimson lips, I became ill at ease and broke off. Perhaps it was because of my fever, but that crimson color seemed to bore into my eyes and make my head ache violently. "But you're wearing so much—In these days how can you use so much make-up without people on the street saying something?"

"Are you already old enough to be noticing a woman's make-up? Lying down like you are, you look exactly like a baby who's just been weaned from the breast."

"What a nuisance you are! Go away!"

She approached me deliberately. I did not want her to see me in my night clothes and pulled the covers up to my neck. Suddenly she stretched out her hand and laid her palm against my forehead. The icy coldness of her hand against my skin was like a stab, and yet it felt good.

"You've got fever. Did you take your temperature?"

"Exactly 103 degrees."

"What you need is an ice bag."

"There's not any ice."

"I'll see to it."

Chieko flounced gaily out of the room, her kimono sleeves flapping against each other, and went downstairs. Soon she returned and sat down in a quiet pose.

"I sent that boy for it."

"Thanks."

I was looking at the ceiling. She picked up the book at my bedside and her cool silken sleeve brushed my cheek.

Suddenly I wanted those cool sleeves. I started to ask her to put them on my forehead, but then I stopped. The room began to become twilit.

"What a slow servant," she said.

A person with fever perceives the passage of time with morbid exactness and I knew it was still too soon for Chieko to be emphasizing that he was slow. A few minutes later she spoke again:

"How slow! What can the boy be doing?"

"He's *not* slow I tell you," I shouted nervously.

"Oh, you poor thing, you're upset. Please close your eyes. Please don't try to outstare the ceiling with such an awful look."

I closed my eyes, and the heat of my eyelids became intense agony. Suddenly I felt something touch my forehead, and with it came a faint breath against my skin. I turned my head and gave a meaningless sigh. At that instant my unusually fevered breath became mingled with hers. My lips were covered by something heavy and greasy. Our teeth crashed together noisily. I was afraid to open my eyes and look. Then she grasped my cheeks firmly between her two cold hands.

After a moment Chieko pulled away and I partially raised myself. There we were glaring at each other in the gloom. It was common knowledge that Chieko's sisters were loose women. Now I realized clearly that she must have the same blood in her veins. But there was an inexplicable and singular feeling of affinity between the passion that was blazing in her and the fever of my illness. I sat up straight and said:

"Once more!"

In this way we continued our endless kisses until the houseboy returned. She kept saying:

"Only kissing, only kissing. . . ."

I did not know whether or not I had experienced any sexual desire during those kisses. However that may be, since what is called a first experience is a kind of sexual feeling in itself, it would probably be useless to draw a distinction in this case. It was no use to try to single out from the drunken emotions of that moment the usual sexual element of the kiss. The important thing was that I had become a "man who knows kisses." And all the time that we were embracing each other I had thought of nothing but Sonoko, exactly like a boy who is served some delicious sweet away from home and immediately wishes he could give some to his younger sister. From then on all my daydreams were focused on the idea of kissing Sonoko. This was my initial and also my most serious miscalculation.

At any rate, as I continued thinking of Sonoko, this first experience gradually became ugly in my eyes. When Chieko called me on the telephone the next day I lied and told her I was returning immediately to the arsenal. I did not even keep our promised rendezvous. I blinded myself to the reality of the fact that I felt unnaturally cold toward her simply because I had derived no pleasure from those kisses, and assured myself instead that they seemed ugly only because I was in love with Sonoko. This was the first time I used my love for Sonoko as a justification for my true feelings.

Sonoko and I exchanged photographs like any boy and girl in their first love affair. She wrote saying she had put mine in a locket and hung it over her breast. But the photograph she sent me was so large that it would only barely have fitted into a brief case. As I could not get it in my pocket, I carried it wrapped in a carrying-cloth. Fearing the factory might burn down with the picture in it, I took it with me whenever I went home.

One night I was on the train returning to the arsenal when the sirens suddenly sounded and the lights were put out. In a few minutes there came the signal to take shelter. I searched in the luggage-rack with groping hands, but the large bundle that I had put there had been stolen, and with it went the carrying-cloth containing Sonoko's picture. Being inherently given to superstition, from that moment I became obsessed with the idea that I must go to see Sonoko quickly.

That air raid of the night of May the twenty-fourth, as destructive as the midnight raid of March the ninth had been, brought me to a final decision. Perhaps my relationship with Sonoko required the miasmal air exhaled by this accumulation of calamities; perhaps that relationship was a sort of chemical compound that could be produced only through the agency of sulphuric acid.

We left the train and took shelter in the many caves that had been dug along a line where the foothills opened onto the plain, and from our shelter we watched the sky over Tokyo turn crimson. From time to time something would explode, throwing a reflection against the sky, and suddenly between the clouds we could see an eerie blue sky, as though it were midday. It was a sliver of blue sky appearing for an instant in the dead of night.

The futile searchlights seemed more like beacons welcoming the enemy planes. They would catch the glittering wings of an enemy plane exactly in the middle of two beams that had crossed momentarily and would then beckon the plane courteously, handing it on from one baton of light to the next, each time nearer Tokyo. Nor was the antiaircraft fire very heavy in those days. The B-29's reached the skies over Tokyo in comfort.

From where we were it was unlikely that anyone could actually distinguish friend from foe in the air battles that were taking place above Tokyo. And yet a chorus of cheers would rise from the crowd of watchers whenever they spotted, against the crimson backdrop, the shadow of a plane that had been hit and was falling. The young workmen were particularly vociferous. The sound of hand-clapping and cheering rang out from the mouths of the scattered tunnels as though in a theater. So far as the spectacle seen from this distance was concerned, it seemed to make no essential difference whether the falling plane was ours or the enemy's. Such is the nature of war. . . .

Instead of going on to the arsenal, as soon as it was light I started home. I had to walk half the length of one of the suburban railway lines, which had been put out of commission, stepping along the still-smouldering ties and crossing the bridges by means of the narrow, half-burned crosswalks. As I got closer home I discovered that nothing had escaped the fire in that whole section of town except our immediate neighborhood, and that our house was untouched. My mother, brother, and sister happened to have been staying there that night, and I found them surprisingly cheerful in spite of the night's fire. They were celebrating their escape by eating some bean jelly, which they had dug up from the place where it had been stored.

Later that day my sixteen-year-old minx of a sister came to my room and said:

"Brother is crazy about a certain somebody, aren't you?"

"Who said any such thing?"

"I know it perfectly well."

"Well, is it wrong to fall in love with someone?"

"Oh no. . . . When will you marry?"

Her words struck deeply within me. My feeling was the same as that of a fugitive from justice when someone, unaware of his guilt, happens to say something to him about his crime.

"Marry? I'm not even thinking about marrying."

"Why, that's wicked! You're crazy about someone without having any intention of marrying her? Oh, that's disgusting. Men really are wicked."

"If you don't leave in a hurry, I'll throw this ink bottle at you."

But even after she had left I could not get her words out of my mind. I started talking to myself: That's right, there could be such a thing in this world as marriage—and children too. Wonder why I forgot this, or at least pretended to forget it. It was only an illusion, telling myself that marriage was too tiny a happiness to exist with the war approaching the final catastrophe. Actually, for me marriage could probably be some very grave happiness. Grave enough—let me see—well, to stir the hairs on my body. . . .

These thoughts also spurred me on to the perverse resolve that I must visit Sonoko at the earliest possible moment. Could this feeling have been love? Was it not instead akin to that strange and passionate form of curiosity a man exhibits toward a fear that dwells in him, to a desire to play with fire?

I had received many invitations to come and visit them, not only from Sonoko, but from her mother and grandmother as well. Not wanting to stay at her aunt's house, I wrote asking Sonoko to reserve a hotel room for me. She inquired at every hotel in N Village, but to no avail. Every hotel had either become a branch office of some government bureau or else been allotted for the detention of foreigners whose countries had now surrendered to the enemy.

A hotel . . . a private room . . . a key . . . the curtained windows . . . gentle resistance . . . mutual agreement to begin hostilities . . . Surely then, surely at that time I would be able to do it. Surely normality would burst into flames within me like a divine revelation. Surely I would be reborn as a different person, as a whole man, just as though suddenly released from the spell of some evil spirit. At that instant I would be able to embrace Sonoko without any hesitation, with all my capacities, and to love her truly. All doubts and misgivings would be utterly wiped away and I would be able to say "I love you" from the bottom of my heart. From that day onward I would be able to walk the street during an air raid and shout "This is my sweetheart" at the top of my voice.

The romantic personality is pervaded with a subtle mistrust of intellectualism, and this fact is often conducive to that immoral action called daydreaming. Contrary to belief, daydreaming is not an intellectual process but rather an escape from intellectualism. . . .

But my dream of the hotel was predestined not to come true. When no room could be found for me at any of the hotels, Sonoko wrote repeatedly urging me to stay with them. I finally agreed. Immediately I was seized with a feeling of relief that resembled exhaustion. No matter how I tried to convince myself that my feeling was one of disappointed resignation, I could not escape the fact that it was nothing more than pure relief.

I left for N Village on June the second. By that time everything at the naval arsenal had become so slipshod that any excuse at all was sufficient to obtain leave.

The train was dirty and empty. Why is it, I wonder, that excepting that one happy instance all my memories of trains during the war are such miserable ones? As I

traveled toward N Village, along with every jolt of the
train came the torment of a childish and pathetic obsession: I was determined that I would not leave without
kissing Sonoko. My determination, however, was different from that feeling filled with pride which comes
when a person struggles to achieve his desire in spite of
timidity: I felt as though I were going thieving. I felt
like a fainthearted apprentice in crime who was being
coerced into becoming a thief by the leader of his gang.
My conscience was pricked by the happiness of being
loved. Or perhaps I was craving some still more decisive
unhappiness.

Sonoko introduced me to her aunt. I wanted to make a
good impression and was trying as hard as I could.
Everyone seemed to be silently asking each other: "Why
did Sonoko ever fall in love with such a fellow? What
a pale bookworm! What on earth can she find to like
about him?"

Having the commendable intention of making everyone think well of me, I did not form an exclusive clique
with Sonoko as I had that time on the train. I helped
her sisters with their English lessons and listened attentively to the grandmother's stories about her days in
Berlin long ago. Oddly enough, it seemed that Sonoko
was all the closer to me at such times. In the presence
of her grandmother or mother I would often exchange
impudent winks with her. At mealtime we would

touch feet under the table. She too gradually became absorbed in this play. Once when I was being bored by the grandmother's yarns, Sonoko leaned against a window through which I could see green leaves under the cloudy sky of the rainy season, and from behind her grandmother, so that only I could see, she held up the locket that hung against her breast and swayed it before my eyes.

How white was the bosom that could be seen above the cresent-shaped neckline of her dress! Startlingly white. Looking at her smile as she leaned against the window, I could understand the reference to the "wanton blood" that dyed Juliet's cheeks. There is a kind of immodesty that becomes only a virgin, differing from the immodesty of a mature woman, and intoxicates the beholder, like a gentle wind. It is a sort of something that is in bad taste but is still somehow cute, for example, like wanting to tickle a baby.

At moments such as these my mind was apt to become intoxicated with sudden happiness. For a long time I had not approached the forbidden fruit called happiness, but it was now tempting me with a melancholy persistence. I felt as though Sonoko were an abyss above which I stood poised.

Thus time passed and only two days remained until I was due to return to the naval arsenal. I still had not fulfilled the obligation of the kiss that I had imposed upon myself.

All the uplands were wrapped in the drizzle of the rainy season. Borrowing a bicycle, I went to the post office to mail a letter. Sonoko was working in a branch of a government office in order to escape being sent away for volunteer labor, but she had promised to meet me at the post office and play truant for the afternoon. On my way there, I passed an abandoned tennis court; it looked lonesome there inside its rusty wire netting, which was dripping from the misty rain. A German boy riding a bicycle passed close beside me, his blond hair and white hands gleaming wet.

I waited a few minutes inside the old-fashioned post office, and during that time the sky became faintly lighter. The rain had ceased. It was but a momentary lull; the clouds did not break, and the light was only platinum colored.

Sonoko brought her bicycle to a halt beyond the glass doors. She was breathing hard, her breasts rising and falling rapidly, but there was a smile on her healthy red cheeks. "Now! sic 'em!" something said within me; and indeed I felt exactly as though I were a hunting dog being encouraged to give chase. I seemed to be acting under the pressure of a moral obligation that some demon had imposed on me. I jumped on my bicycle and side by side with Sonoko went riding the length of the main street.

We rode on out of the village and through a grove of trees—firs, maples, and silver birch, all dripping bright raindrops. Sonoko's hair was beautiful as it streamed behind her in the wind. Her strong thighs rose and fell smartly as she pedaled. She looked like life itself. At the entrance to a golf course, which was no longer being used, we got off our bicycles and walked along a wet lane bordering the fairway.

I was as tense as a new recruit. Over there is a clump of trees, I told myself. Its shadows are exactly right. It's about fifty paces away. After twenty more paces I'll begin saying something to her to relieve the tension. And during the remaining thirty paces it'll be all right just to keep up some ordinary conversation. The fiftieth pace—we'll put down the bicycle stands and stop to look at the view toward the mountains. Then I'll put my hand on her shoulder. I can even say in a low voice: "Being here like this is something I've dreamed about." Then she'll make some innocent reply. I'll tighten the hand I have on her shoulder, swinging her around toward me. And then the only technique I'll need is just the same as that time with Chieko. . . .

I swore to play my role faithfully. It had nothing to do with either love or desire. . . .

Sonoko was actually in my arms. Breathing quickly, she blushed red as fire and closed her eyes. Her lips were childishly beautiful. But they aroused no desire in me. And yet I kept hoping that something would happen within me at any moment—surely when I actually kiss her, surely then I will discover my normality, my unfeigned love.

The machine was rushing onward. No one could stop it.

I covered her lips with mine. A second passed. There is not the slightest sensation of pleasure. Two seconds. It is just the same. Three seconds. . . . I understood everything.

I drew away from her and stood for an instant regarding her with sad eyes. If she had looked into my eyes at that instant she would surely have received a hint as to the indefinable nature of my love for her. Whatever it was, no one could have asserted positively whether such a love was or was not humanly possible. But Sonoko, overwhelmed with bashfulness and innocent joy, kept her eyes cast down, doll-like.

Saying not a word, I took her arm, as though she were an invalid, and we began walking toward the bicycles.

I must flee, I kept telling myself. Without a moment's delay I must flee. I was in a panic. And to keep from arousing suspicion by looking as glum as I felt, I pretended to be even more cheerful than usual. The success of my little ruse placed me in an even more difficult position: during the evening meal my happy looks coincided so well with Sonoko's deep absent-mindedness that everyone drew the obvious conclusion.

Sonoko looked even younger and fresher than usual. There had always been a storybook quality about her face and figure. Now there was an air about her that reminded one exactly how a storybook maiden looks and acts when in love. Seeing her naïve maidenly heart exposed before me in this way, I was only too clearly aware that I had had no right to hold such a beautiful spirit in my arms, and no matter how I attempted to continue my pretense at gaiety, my conversation flagged. Noticing this, Sonoko's mother expressed some anxiety concerning my health. Sonoko jumped to the hasty conclusion that she knew exactly what I was thinking, and in order to rally me, she shook her locket in my direction, giving the signal of "Don't worry." In spite of myself, I smiled back at her.

The adults at the table showed a row of faces half-shocked and half-annoyed by our audacious exchange of smiles. Suddenly I realized that the imaginations behind this row of faces were already hard at work calling up pictures of a future for the two of us together, and again I was struck with terror.

Next day we went again to the same spot by the golf course. I noticed a clump of wild flowers that we had trampled underfoot upon departing—yellow camomiles, relics of our yesterday. Today the grass was dry.

Habit is a horrible thing. I repeated the kiss for which I had so repented. But this time it was like the kiss one gives his little sister. And by just this much did it savor all the more of immorality.

"I wonder when I'll see you next," she said.

"Well," I answered, "if the Americans don't make their landing near the arsenal I can get leave again in about a month." I was hoping—no, it was more than mere hope, it was a superstitious certainty—that during that month the Americans would surely land at S Bay and we would all be sent out as a student army to die to the last man, or else that a monstrous bomb, such as no one had ever imagined, would kill me, no matter where I might be taking shelter. . . . Could this have been a premonition of the atom bomb which was soon to fall?

Then we went toward a slope bathed in sunlight. Two silver birch were shading the slope, looking like gentlehearted sisters. Sonoko, walking along with downcast eyes, broke the silence:

"When we meet next, what sort of present will you bring me?"

"As for a present that I could bring in these days," I answered in desperation, pretending not to understand her meaning, "about the best I could do would be a defective plane or a muddy shovel."

"I don't mean something that has a shape."

"H'm, what could it be?" The more I feigned ignorance the more I was being driven into a corner. "It's a real riddle, isn't it? I'll puzzle it out at leisure on the train going back."

"Yes, please do." Her tone of voice was a strange

combination of self-possession and dignity. "I want you to promise you'll bring the gift."

Sonoko had emphasized the word promise, and there was nothing I could do to defend myself except continue my bluff of cheerfulness:

"Good!" I said patronizingly, "let's lock fingers on it."

We locked our fingers together in that way children have for sealing their promises. The gesture seemed innocent enough, but suddenly I was beset with a fear I had known in childhood. I remembered how children said your finger would rot away if you broke a promise after you'd locked fingers on it. And my fear had an even more real reason: even if she did not say so, it was clear that Sonoko's talk of a present was a request for a marriage proposal. My fear was like that which a child feels all about him at night when he is afraid to go alone down a dark passage.

That night at bedtime Sonoko came to the door of my room and, hiding herself partially behind the curtain hanging there, begged me poutingly to stay one day longer. I could only stare at her as though astonished by something. My entire calculation, which I had thought so very exact, had been destroyed by the discovery of that error I had made at the very outset, and consequently I had no idea how to analyze the feelings I had now when I looked at Sonoko.

"Must you really go?"

"Yes, it's a must."

I almost felt happy as I gave the answer. Again the machinery of deception had begun to work within me, superficially at first. My feeling of happiness was actually nothing but the emotion one feels upon escaping a great danger, but I interpreted it as arising out of a feeling of superiority toward Sonoko, out of the knowledge that I now possessed new power to tantalize her.

Self-deception was now my last ray of hope. A person who has been seriously wounded does not demand that the emergency bandages that save his life be clean. I arrested my bleeding with the bandages of self-deception, with which I was at least already familiar, and thought of nothing but running to the hospital. I purposely described that slipshod arsenal to Sonoko as the strictest of barracks, insisting that if I did not return to it the next day I'd probably be put in a military prison. . . .

The morning of my departure had arrived and I found myself gazing intently at Sonoko—like a traveler looking for the last time upon a scene he is about to leave. I now realized that everything was over—even though the people around me were thinking that everything was just beginning—even though I too was wanting to deceive myself and surrender to the atmosphere of gentle vigilance with which her family surrounded me.

And yet Sonoko's air of tranquillity made me feel

uneasy. She was helping me pack my bag, searching the room to see if I had forgotten something. After a time she stopped before a window and stared out it, not moving. Today again there was nothing to be seen distinctly except the cloudy sky and the fresh green leaves. The invisible passage of a squirrel had set a branch to swaying. As I looked at Sonoko's back something about her posture made it abundantly clear that she was quietly but childishly waiting. Given my methodical ways, I could no more have ignored this than I can endure leaving a room without closing the closet doors. I walked up behind her and embraced her gently.

"You will come again, without fail, won't you?"

She spoke easily, in a tone of complete confidence. It somehow sounded as though she had confidence not so much in me as in something deeper, something beyond me. Her shoulders were not shaking. The lace on her blouse was rising and falling as though proudly.

"H'm, perhaps so, if I'm still alive."

I was disgusted with myself as I spoke the words. Intellectually, I would have preferred by far to be saying: "Of course I'll come! Nothing could keep me from coming to you. Never doubt it. Aren't you the girl who's going to be my wife?"

At every turn this sort of curious contradiction cropped up between my intellectual views and my emotions. I knew that what made me adopt such lukewarm attitudes—like that "H'm, perhaps so"—was not some fault in my character that I could change, but was the work of something that had existed even before I had had any hand in the matter. In short, I knew clearly that it was not my fault.

But for this very reason I had formed the habit of treating those parts of my character that were in any way my responsibility to exhortations so wholesome and sensible as to be comical. As a part of my system of self-discipline, dating from childhood, I constantly told myself it would be better to die than become a lukewarm person, an unmanly person, a person who does not clearly know his likes and dislikes, a person who wants only to be loved without knowing how to love. This exhortation of course had a possible applicability to the parts of my character for which I was to blame, but so far as the other parts were concerned, the parts for which I was not to blame, it was an impossible requirement from the beginnnig. Thus, in the present case even the strength of a Samson would not have been sufficient to make me adopt a manly and unequivocal attitude toward Sonoko.

So then, this image of a lukewarm man that Sonoko was now seeing, this thing that appeared to be my character, aroused my disgust, made my entire existence seem worthless, and tore my self-confidence into shreds. I was made to distrust both my will and my character, or at least, so far as my will was concerned, I could not believe it was anything but a fake. On the other hand, this way of thinking that placed such emphasis upon the will was in itself an exaggeration amounting almost to fantasy. Even a normal person cannot govern his behavior by will alone. No matter how normal I might have been, there certainly might have been a reason somewhere for doubting whether Sonoko and I were perfectly matched at every point for a happy married life, some reason that would have justified even that normal me in answering "H'm, perhaps so." But I had deliberately acquired the habit of closing my eyes even to such obvious assumptions, just as though I did not want to miss a single opportunity for tormenting myself. . . . This is a trite device, often adopted by persons who, cut off from all other means of escape, retreat into the safe haven of regarding themselves as objects of tragedy. . . .

"Don't worry," Sonoko said in a quiet voice. "You won't be killed. You won't be even slightly hurt. Every night I pray to the Lord Jesus for you, and my prayers are always answered."

"You're very devout, aren't you? That's probably the reason you have such peace of mind. It's enough to make me afraid."

"Why?" she asked, looking up at me with wise black eyes.

I was caught between her glance and her innocent question, both as free of doubt as is the dew, and I was overcome with confusion. I could think of no answer to make. Until now I had felt a strong desire to shake this girl, who seemed to have gone to sleep within her peace of mind, to shake her till she awakened. But instead it was the gaze of her eyes that had awakened something that had been sleeping within me. . . .

It was time for Sonoko's younger sisters to go to school and they came to take their leave. The smallest sister barely touched my palm with her hand as she said good-bye, and then fled outdoors, carrying a crimson lunch box with a gold-colored buckle. Just at that moment the sun happened to shine through the trees and I saw her wave her lunch box high over her head.

Both the grandmother and mother had come along to see me off, so my parting with Sonoko at the station was casual and innocent. We jested with each other and acted nonchalant. The train came soon and I took a seat by a window. My only thought was a prayer that the train would leave quickly. . . .

A clear voice called to me from an unexpected direction. It was certainly Sonoko's voice, but accustomed as I had become to it, I was startled to hear it as a fresh, distant cry. The realization that it was Sonoko's voice streamed into my heart like morning sunlight. I turned my eyes in the direction from which it came. Sonoko had slipped in through the porters' gate and was clinging to the black wooden railing bordering the platform. A mass of lace on her blouse overflowed from her checked bolero and fluttered in the breeze. Her vivacious eyes stared widely at me. The train began to move. Her slightly heavy lips seemed to be forming words, and in just that way she passed out of my view.

Sonoko! Sonoko! I repeated the name to myself with each sway of the train. It sounded unutterably mysterious. Sonoko! Sonoko! With each repetition my heart felt heavier, at each throb of her name a cutting, punishing weariness grew deeper within me. The pain I was feeling was crystal clear, but of such a unique and incomprehensible nature that I could not have explained it even if I had tried. It was so far off the beaten path of ordinary human emotions that I even had difficulty in recognizing it as pain. If I should try to describe it, I could only say it was a pain like that of a person who waits one bright midday for the roar of the noon-gun and, when the time for the gun's sounding has passed in silence, tries to discover the waiting emptiness somewhere in the blue sky. His is the rending impatience of waiting for a longed-for thing that is overdue, the horrible doubt that it may never come after all. He is the only man in the world who knows that the noon-gun did not sound promptly at noon.

"It's all over, it's all over," I muttered to myself. My grief resembled that of a fainthearted student who has failed an examination: I made a mistake! I made a mistake! Simply because I didn't solve that X, everything was wrong. If only I'd solved that X at the beginning, everything would have been all right. If only I had used deductive methods like everyone else to solve the mathematics of life. To be half-clever was the worst thing I could have done. I alone depended upon the inductive method, and for that simple reason I failed.

My mental turmoil was so apparent that the two passengers who sat in the facing seat began eyeing me suspiciously. One of them was a Red Cross nurse wearing a dark-blue uniform, and the other a poor farm-woman who seemed to be the nurse's mother. Becoming conscious of their stares, I glanced at the nurse and saw a fat girl, with a complexion as red as a winter-cherry. I surprised her looking directly at me; to cover her confusion she began to coax her mother:

"Please, I'm *so* hungry."

"No, it's too early yet."

"But I'm hungry, I tell you. Please, please."

"Don't be so demanding."

But at last the mother yielded and got out their lunch box. The poverty of its contents made their lunch even more dreadful than the food we received at the arsenal. There was only boiled rice, heavily mixed with taro-root and garnished with two slices of pickled radish, but the girl began eating it with gusto.

Somehow the habit of eating had never before appeared so ridiculous to me, and I rubbed my eyes.

Presently I realized that my point of view came from having completely lost the desire to live.

When I arrived at the house in the suburbs that night I seriously contemplated suicide for the first time in my life. But as I thought about it, the idea became exceedingly tiresome, and I finally decided it would be a ludicrous business. I had an inherent dislike of admitting defeat. Moreover, I told myself, there's no need for me to take such decisive action myself, not when I'm surrounded by such a bountiful harvest of so many types of death—death in an air raid, death at one's post of duty, death in the military service, death on the battlefield, death from being run over, death from disease—surely my name has already been entered in the list for one of these: a criminal who has been sentenced to death does not commit suicide. No—no matter how I considered it, the season was not auspicious for suicide. Instead I was waiting for something to do me the favor of killing me. And this, in the final analysis, is the same as to say that I was waiting for something to do me the favor of keeping me alive.

Two days after my return to the arsenal I received an impassioned letter from Sonoko. There was no doubt that she was truly in love. I felt jealous. Mine was the unbearable jealousy a cultured pearl must feel toward a genuine one. Or can there be such a thing in this world as a man who is jealous of the woman who loves him, precisely because of her love? . . .

She wrote that after parting from me at the station she got on her bicycle and went to work. But she was so absent-minded that her fellow workers asked if she felt well. She made many errors in filing the papers. Then she went home to lunch, but as she was returning to work after lunch she made a detour by way of the golf course, where she stopped. She looked around and saw where the yellow camomile lay trampled just as we had left it. Then, as the fog dissolved, she saw the flanks of the volcano shining brightly with the color of burnt ochre, looking as though the mountain had been washed. She also saw traces of dark fog arising from the gorges in the mountain, and saw the two silver birch, like loving sisters, their leaves trembling as with some faint premonition. . . .

And at that very time I had been on the train, cudgeling my brain for a way to escape the very love which I myself had implanted in Sonoko! . . . And yet there were moments in which I felt reassured, surrendering myself to a plea of self-justification that, however pitiful, was probably nearest the truth. This was the plea that I had to escape from her for the very reason that I did love her.

I continued writing Sonoko frequent letters, and while I was careful not to say anything that might develop the matter further, at the same time I used a tone that would reveal no cooling off on my part. Within less than a month she wrote telling me that they were all going to visit Kusano again at the regiment near Tokyo to which he had been transferred. Weakness urged me to go with them. Strangely enough, even though I had resolved so firmly to escape from her, still I was irresistibly drawn to another meeting.

And when I did meet her I found that I had completely changed, while she remained just the same as ever. It had become impossible now for me to make a single joke. Sonoko and Kusano, and even her mother and grandmother, noticed the change in me, but they ascribed it to nothing more than my sincerity of purpose. During the visit Kusano made a remark to me which, even though spoken with his usual gentleness, made me tremble with apprehension:

"In a few days I'll be sending you a rather important letter. Be on the lookout for it, will you?" . . .

A week later I went to the house in the suburbs where my family were, and found his letter had arrived. It was written in that handwriting so characteristic of him, revealing in its very immaturity the sincerity of his friendship:

". . . All the family is concerned about you and Sonoko. I have been appointed ambassador plentipotentiary in the matter. What I have to say is brief—I simply want to ask how you feel about it. Naturally Sonoko is counting on you, and everyone else is too. My mother has apparently even begun thinking about when the ceremony should be. Maybe it's too early for that, but I imagine it would be all right to go ahead and fix a date for the engagement now. But of course we're only guessing. That's why I want to ask how you feel about it. The family would like to settle everything, including making arrangements with your family, just as soon as we hear from you. But I certainly don't mean to force you to take any step you're not ready to take. Just tell me how you really feel and I'll quit worrying. Even if your answer is no, I'll never hold it against you or be angry, nor will it affect our friendship. Of course I'll be delighted if it's yes, but my feelings won't be hurt even if it's no. What I want is your frank answer, freely given. I sincerely hope you'll answer without any feeling of compulsion or obligation. As your very good friend I'm awaiting your answer. . . ."

I was thunderstruck. I looked around, feeling that someone might have been watching me as I read the letter.

I had never dreamed that this could happen. I had failed to take into account the fact that Sonoko and her family might have an attitude toward the war markedly different from my own. I was a student, still under twenty-one, and working in an airplane factory; moreover, having grown up during a series of wars, I had thought too much of the romantic sway of war. Actually, however, even during such times of violent disaster as these to which the war had now brought us, the magnetic needle of human affairs still remained pointing in the same direction as always. And up to now even I had thought I was in love. So why had I failed to realize that the everyday affairs and responsibilities of life went on even in wartime?

As I reread Kusano's letter, however, a strange, faint smile came playing about my lips, and at last a quite ordinary feeling of superiority rose in me. I'm a conqueror, I told myself. A person who has never known happiness has no right to scorn it. But I give an appearance of happiness in which no one can detect any flaw, and so have as much right to scorn it as anyone else.

Even though my heart was filled with uneasiness and unspeakable grief, I put a brazen, cynical smile upon my lips. I told myself that all I had to do was clear one small hurdle. All I had to do was to regard all the past few months as absurd; to decide that from the beginning I'd never been in love with a girl called Sonoko, not with such a chit of a girl; to believe that I'd been prompted by a trifling passion (liar!) and had deceived her. Then there'd be no reason why I couldn't refuse her. Surely a mere kiss didn't obligate me! . . .

I was elated with the conclusion to which my thoughts had brought me: "I'm not in love with Sonoko."

What a splendid thing! I've become a man who can entice a woman without even loving her, and then, when love blazes up in her, abandon her without thinking twice about it. How far I am from being the upright and virtuous honor student I appear to be. . . . And yet I could not have been ignorant of the fact that there is no such thing as a libertine who abandons a woman without first achieving his purpose. But I ignored any such thoughts. I had acquired the habit of closing my ears completely, like an obstinate old woman, to anything I did not want to hear.

The only thing needed now was to devise a way to get out of the marriage. I set about the task exactly as though I were a jealous lover scheming to prevent a marriage between the girl he loved and someone else.

I opened the window and called my mother.

The large vegetable garden was bright in the strong summer sunlight. Rows of tomatoes and eggplants lifted their parched leaves toward the sun, defiantly, sharply. The sun kept pouring its scorching rays thickly over the strong-veined leaves. As far as the eye could reach the dark abundance of vegetable life was crushed beneath the brilliance that fell upon the garden. Beyond the garden there was a grove of trees around a shrine that turned its face gloomily in my direction. And beyond that there was low land, across which electric trains passed unseen from time to time, filling the countryside with vibrations. After each heedless passage of an upthrust trolley pole the cable was left swaying lazily, flashing in the sunlight.

In response to my call a large straw hat with a blue-ribbon streamer rose from the middle of the vegetable garden. It was my mother. The straw hat my uncle was wearing—he was my mother's elder brother—remained motionless, bent over like a drooping sunflower, without once turning in my direction.

With her present way of life my mother's complexion had become somewhat tanned and I could see the flash of her white teeth as she moved toward me. When she was close enough to be heard, she called out to me in a high-pitched childlike voice:

"What is it? If you want to tell me something, come out here."

"It's something important. You come here a minute."

My mother approached slowly, as though protesting. She was carrying a basket heaped with ripe tomatoes. Reaching the house, she put the basket on the window sill and asked what I wanted.

I did not show her the letter, but told her briefly what it said. As I was speaking I forgot why I had called her; it may have been that I was chattering on simply to convince myself. I told her that whoever became my wife would certainly have a hard time living in the same house with my nervous and fussy father, and yet there was no hope of having a separate house in such times as these. Moreover, there would probably be all the difference in the world between the ways of our old-fashioned family and what I described as Sonoko's vivacious, easygoing family. And as for me, I didn't want the worry of taking on the responsibility of a wife so soon. . . . I gave all these various trite objections with a cool air, hoping my mother would agree and obstinately oppose any thought of my marrying. But she was as calm and indulgent as ever.

"That's a funny way to talk," she broke in, as though giving little thought to the matter. "So then, how do you really feel? Do you love her, or don't you?"

"Of course, I also—well—" I mumbled. "But I was not so serious as all that. I only meant it half in fun. Then she became serious and got me into deep water."

"Then there's no problem is there? The sooner you straighten it out the better for both of you. After all, the letter is only trying to find out how you feel about it. You'd better just send a plain answer—So I'll be getting back. Everything's all right now, isn't it?"

"H'm," I answered and gave a little sigh.

My mother went as far as the bamboo gate, around which corn was growing. Then she came running back nervously to the window where I was. Her expression now was somehow changed.

"Listen, about what we were just saying—" She looked at me with an odd expression, as though she were a strange woman looking at me for the first time, "—about Sonoko. You—she—if you've—well—"

Catching her meaning, I laughed and said:

"Don't be foolish, Mother." I felt as though I had never before laughed so bitterly. "Do you really think I did any such thing? Do you trust me so little?"

"Oh, I knew it. I just had to make sure." She resumed her cheerful countenance, hiding her embarrassment. "That's what mothers are for—to worry about such things. Don't worry. I trust you." . . .

That night I wrote a letter of indirect refusal, which sounded artificial even to me. I wrote that it was a very sudden thing and that as yet my feelings had not gone quite that far.

On my way back to the arsenal next morning, I stopped by the post office to mail the letter. The woman at the special-delivery window looked suspiciously at my trembling hands. I stared at my letter as she took it up in her rough, dirty hands and stamped it swiftly. I found comfort in seeing my unhappiness handled in such an efficient, businesslike manner.

The enemy planes had changed their targets now and were attacking smaller cities and towns. It seemed as though life had momentarily been delivered from all danger. Views favoring surrender had become fashionable among the students. One of our young assistant professors began making suggestive allusions to peace, trying to curry favor with the students. Seeing the smug bulge of his short nose as he gave voice to the most skeptical views, I thought: "Don't you try to fool me." And on the other hand I also despised the fanatics who still believed in victory. It was all the same to me whether the war was won or lost. The only thing I wanted was to start a new life.

While visiting the house in the suburbs I was taken with a high fever, the cause of which was unknown. As I lay staring at the ceiling, which seemed to revolve feverishly, I muttered Sonoko's name continuously to myself as though it were a sacred scripture. When I was finally able to get out of bed I heard the news of the destruction of Hiroshima.

It was our last chance. People were saying that Tokyo would be next. Wearing white shirt and shorts, I walked about the streets. The people had reached the limits of desperation and were now going about their affairs with cheerful faces. From one moment to the next nothing happened. Everywhere there was an air of cheerful excitement. It was just as though one was continuing to blow up an already bulging toy balloon, wondering: "Will it burst now? will it burst now?" And yet from moment to moment nothing happened. This state of things lasted for almost ten days. If it had gone on any longer, there would have been nothing to do but go crazy.

Then one day some trim planes threaded their way through the stupid antiaircraft fire and rained propaganda leaflets down from the summer sky. The leaflets contained news of the surrender proposals. That evening my father came straight from his office to the house in the suburbs. He came in through the garden and spoke immediately, sitting down on the veranda.

"Listen," he said, "that propaganda is true." He showed me a copy of the original English text, which he had obtained from a reliable source.

I took the copy into my hands, but even before I had had time to read it I had already grasped the reality of the news. It was not the reality of defeat. Instead, for me—for me alone—it meant that fearful days were beginning. It meant that, whether I would or no, and despite everything that had deceived me into believing such a day would never come, the very next day I must begin that "everyday life" of a member of human society. How the mere words made me tremble!

CHAPTER FOUR

Contrary to my expectations, that everyday life which I feared showed not the slightest sign of beginning. Instead, it felt as though the country were engaged in a sort of civil war, and people seemed to be giving even less thought to "tomorrow" than they had during the real war.

The schoolmate who had lent me his university uniform was discharged from the army, and I returned his uniform to him. Then for a time I had the illusion that I had been liberated from memories, from memories of all my past.

My sister died. I derived a superficial peace-of-mind from the discovery that even I could shed tears.

Sonoko became formally engaged and was married shortly after my sister's death. My reaction to this event

—would I be right in describing it as the feeling of having had a burden lifted from my shoulders? I pretended to myself that I was pleased. I boasted to myself that this was only natural since it was I who had done the jilting and not she.

I had long insisted upon interpreting the things that Fate forced me to do as victories of my own will and intelligence, and now this bad habit had grown into a sort of frenzied arrogance. In the nature of what I was calling my intelligence there was a touch of something illegitimate, a touch of the sham pretender who has been placed on the throne by some freak chance. This dolt of a usurper could not foresee the revenge that would inevitably be wreaked upon his stupid despotism.

I passed the next year with vague and optimistic feelings. There were my law studies, perfunctorily performed, and my automatic goings and comings between university and home. . . . I was not paying attention to anything, nor was anything paying attention to me. I had acquired a worldly-wise smile like that of a young priest. I had the feeling of being neither alive nor dead. It seemed that my former desire for the natural and spontaneous suicide of death in war had been completely eradicated, and forgotten.

True pain can only come gradually. It is exactly like tuberculosis in that the disease has already progressed to a critical stage before the patient becomes aware of its symptoms.

One day I stopped in a bookstore, where new publications were gradually beginning to reappear, and happened to take down a translation in a crude paper binding. It was a collection of wordy essays by a French writer. I opened the book at random and one line on the page burned itself into my eyes. An acute feeling of uneasiness forced me to close the book and return it to the shelf.

On my way to school the next morning something suddenly possessed me to stop by the same bookstore, which was near the main gate of the university, and buy the book I had looked at the day before. During a lecture on the Civil Code, I took the book out stealthily and, laying it beside my open notebook, hunted up the same line. It now gave me an even more vivid feeling of unease than it had the day before:

> *. . . The measure of a woman's power is the degree of suffering with which she can punish her lover. . . .*

I had one friend at the university with whom I was on familiar terms. His family owned a long-established confectioner's shop. At first glance, he appeared to be an uninteresting, diligent student; the cynical tone of voice he used toward people and life, together with the fact that he had a frail build similar to mine, aroused a sympathetic attraction in me. But while my cynicism came from a desire for creating an impression and for self-defense, the same attitude in him seemed to be rooted in some firmer feeling of self-confidence. I wondered where he got his confidence. After a time he guessed that I was still a virgin and, speaking with a mixture of overwhelming superiority and self-contempt, confessed that he had been visiting brothels. Then he sounded out my feelings on the subject.

". . . So if you'd like to go sometime, just give me a call. I'll take you any time."

"H'm. If I want to go, all right. . . . Maybe. . . . I'll make up my mind soon," I answered.

He seemed abashed, and yet triumphant. His expression reflected my own feeling of shame; it was as though he thought he completely understood my present state of mind and was being reminded of the time when he himself had experienced exactly the same feelings. I felt harassed. It was that restless feeling, already well established in me, of wanting actually to have the feelings with which I was credited.

Prudery is a form of selfishness, a means of self-protection made necessary by the strength of one's own desires. But my true desires were so secret that they did not allow even this form of self-indulgence. And at the same time any imaginary desires—that is, my simple and abstract curiosity concerning women—allowed me such a cold freedom that there was almost no room for this selfishness in them either. There is no virtue in curiosity. In fact, it might even be the most immoral desire a man can possess.

I devised a pathetic secret exercise. It consisted of testing my desire by staring fixedly at pictures of naked women. . . . As may be easily imagined, my desire answered neither yes or no. Upon indulging in that bad habit of mine, I would try to discipline my desire, first by refraining from my usual daydreams, and later by forcibly calling up mental images of women in the most obscene poses. At times it seemed my efforts were successful. But there was a falseness about this success that seemed to grind my heart into powder.

At last I decided it was sink or swim. I telephoned my friend and asked him to meet me one Sunday afternoon at five o'clock at a certain teashop. This was toward the middle of January in the second year after the end of the war.

"So you finally made up your mind?" He laughed delightedly over the telephone. "All right, I'll be there. And listen—I'll be there for sure. I won't forgive you if you don't come." . . .

After I had hung up, his laughing voice still echoed in my ears. I was aware that I had been able to counter his laughter with nothing better than an invisible, twisted smile. And yet I felt a ray of hope or, better said, a superstitious belief. It was a dangerous superstition. Only vanity makes people take risks. In my case it was the commonplace vanity of not wanting to be known as a virgin at the age of twenty-two.

Now that I think of it, it was on my birthday that I thus steeled myself for the test. . . .

We stared at each other as though each was trying to probe the other's mind. Today my friend too realized that either a serious face or a broad grin would look equally absurd, and he exhaled cigarette smoke rapidly from his expressionless lips. After a few words of greeting he began talking impersonaly about the poor quality of the confections served at this shop. I was scarcely listening to him and broke into his remarks:

"I wonder if you've made up your mind also. I wonder if a fellow who takes someone to such a place for the first time becomes a lifelong friend or a lifelong enemy."

"Don't scare me. You know what a coward I am. I wouldn't know how to play the part of a lifelong enemy."

"It's good that you know even that much about yourself." I deliberately talked down to him, making a show of bravado.

"Well, then," he said, looking as grave as a committee chairman, "we ought to go somewhere and have something to drink. It's a little too much for a beginner if he's sober."

"No, I don't want to drink." I felt my cheeks grow cold. "I'm going without taking a single drink. I have nerve enough without it."

In quick succession there came a ride on a gloomy streetcar and a gloomy elevated, an unfamiliar station, an unfamiliar street, a corner where shabby tenements stood in rows, and purple and red lights under which the women's faces looked swollen. The customers walked along the clammy, thawing street, passing each other in silence, their footfalls as hushed as though they were barefoot. I felt not the slightest desire. It was nothing but my feeling of uneasiness that goaded me on, exactly as though I were a child pleading for a mid-afternoon snack.

"Any place will do," I said. "Any place will do, I tell you." I felt as though I wanted to turn and flee from the artificially husky voices of the women saying: "Stop a minute, honey; wait just a minute, honey. . . ."

"The girls in this house are dangerous. . . . You like that one? God, what a face! But at least that house is fairly safe."

"The face doesn't make any difference," I said.

"All right then, just to be different I'll take the pretty one. Don't hold it against me later."

At our approach the two women jumped up as though some devil had taken possession of them. We went in the house, which was so small that our heads seemed to touch the ceiling as we entered. Giving a smile that revealed her gold teeth and gums, the spindly one with a country accent took me off to a tiny three-mat room.

A sense of duty made me embrace her. Holding her in my arms, I was about to kiss her. Her heavy shoulders began shaking crazily with laughter.

"Don't do thaaat! You'll get lipstick on you. This here's the way."

The prostitute opened her big mouth, its gold teeth framed by lipstick, and produced her sturdy tongue like a stick. Following her example, I stuck out my tongue also. The tips of our tongues touched. . . .

Perhaps I will not be understood when I say there is a numbness that resembles fierce pain. I felt my entire body becoming paralyzed with just such a pain, a pain that was intense, but still could not be felt at all. I dropped my head onto the pillow.

Ten minutes later there was no doubt of my incapacity. My knees were shaking with shame.

I assumed that my friend had no suspicion of what had happened, and surprisingly enough, during the next few days I surrendered myself to the drab feelings of convalescence. I was like a person who has been suffering an unknown disease in an agony of fear: just learning the name of his disease, even though it is an incurable one, gives him a surprising feeling of temporary relief. He knows well, though, that the relief is only temporary. Moreover, in his heart he foresees a still more inescapable hopelessness, which, by its very nature, will give a more permanent feeling of relief. I too had probably come to expect a blow that it would be even more impossible to parry, or to say it another way, a more inescapable feeling of relief.

During the following weeks I met my friend at school many times, but neither of us ever referred to the incident. About a month later he came to visit me one evening, accompanied by another student, a mutual acquaintance of ours. This was T, a great ladies' man, full of vanity and always boasting that he could make any girl in only fifteen minutes. In no time our conversation descended to the inevitable theme.

"I just can't get along without it any more—I simply can't control myself," T said, looking closely at me. "If any of my friends were impotent I'd really envy them. More than that, I'd bow down to them."

My friend saw that my face had changed color, and he turned the conversation to a new subject, addressing T:

"You promised to lend me a book by Marcel Proust, remember? Is it interesting?"

"I'll say it's interesting. Proust was a *sodomite*"—he used the foreign word. "He had affairs with footmen."

"What's a sodomite?" I asked. I realized that by feigning ignorance I was desperately pawing the air, clutching at this little question for support and trying to find some clue to their thoughts, some indication that they did not suspect my disgrace.

"A sodomite's a sodomite. Didn't you know? It's a *danshokuka*."

"Oh . . . but I never heard Proust was that way."

I could tell that my voice was quivering. To have looked offended would have been the same as giving my companions proof positive. I was ashamed of being able to maintain such a disgraceful outward show of equanimity. It was obvious that my friend had smelled out my secret. Somehow it seemed to me that he was doing all he could to avoid looking at my face.

My cursed visitors finally left at eleven o'clock, and I shut myself up for a sleepless night in my room. I cried sobbingly until at last those visions reeking with blood came to comfort me. And then I surrendered myself to them, to those deplorably brutal visions, my most intimate friends.

Some diversion was essential. I began dropping in frequently at the gatherings that took place at the house of an old friend, knowing that they would leave nothing in my mind but the memory of idle conversation and a blank aftertaste. I went there because the people of smart society who came to those parties, unlike my classmates, seemed surprisingly friendly and easy to know. They included several stylishly affected young ladies, a famous soprano, a budding lady pianist, and various young wives who had only recently married. There would be dancing, a little drinking, and the playing of silly games, including a slightly erotic form of tag. Sometimes the parties would last until dawn.

In the early hours of the morning we would often find ourselves falling asleep as we danced. Then to keep awake we would play a game, scattering cushions about the floor and dancing around them in a circle until the phonograph was suddenly stopped. At this signal we would sit down on the pillows two by two, and whoever failed to find a seat would have to do a stunt. Great excitement was created by the dancers' throwing themselves down in heaps upon the cushions. As the game progressed, being repeated many times, even the women seemed to become careless of their appearance.

Perhaps it was because she was a little intoxicated, but I remember how I once saw the prettiest of the girls laughing excitedly, not noticing that in the confusion of falling to a cushion her skirt had been pulled up far above her thighs. The flesh of her thighs gleamed whitely. If this had happened a short time before, I probably would have imitated the way other young men shy away from their own desire in such a situation, and using all my skill at playing a part that was never forgotten a single moment, would have instantly averted my eyes. But since that certain day I had changed. Without the slightest feeling of shame—that is, without the slightest shame at my innate shamelessness—I stared at those white thighs as calmly as though I were examining some piece of inanimate matter.

Suddenly I was struck by the astringent pain that

comes from staring too long at something. The pain proclaimed: You're not human. You're a being who is incapable of social intercourse. You're nothing but a creature, non-human and somehow strangely pathetic.

Fortunately, the time for preparing for the civil-service examinations was at hand and I had to devote all my energies to dry-as-dust studying for them. This automatically enabled me, both physically and mentally, to keep more tormenting matters at a distance. But even this distraction was effective for only a short time at the beginning.

The sense of failure which that night had aroused in me gradually returned, spreading into every corner of my life. I became depressed. For days on end I would be unable to turn my hand to anything. The need to prove to myself that I had some sort of potency seemed to become more urgent each day. It seemed that I could not go on living without some such proof. And yet nowhere could I discover a clue to the realization of my inherent perversity. There was no opportunity here for satisfying my abnormal desires, not even in their mildest form.

Spring came, and a frantic nervousness was built up behind my façade of tranquillity. It seemed as though the season itself bore me a grudge, expressing its hostility in its dust-laden winds. If an automobile almost grazed me, I would mentally berate it in a loud voice, saying: "Well, why don't you go on and run over me!"

I delighted in the strenuous study and Spartan existence I had imposed upon myself. At odd moments in my studying I would go out for a walk, and often I became aware that people were looking questioningly at my bloodshot eyes. Even when an observer might have thought I was heaping very diligent day on diligent day, actually I was only learning the gnawing fatigue of sloppiness, dissipation, utterly rotten laziness, and a way of life that knew no tomorrow. But then one afternoon toward the end of spring I was on a streetcar and suddenly felt a pure throbbing of the heart that seemed to take my breath.

It was because, looking between the standing passengers, I had caught a glimpse of Sonoko sitting on the opposite side of the car. There beneath her childlike eyebrows I could see her eyes, sincere and modest, with their indescribably profound gentleness. I was on the point of getting to my feet when one of the passengers let go his strap and began moving toward the exit. Then the girl's face became entirely visible. It was not Sonoko.

My heart was still clamoring. It was easy to explain to myself that those heart throbs were due simply to surprise or else to a guilty conscience, but even such an explanation could not destroy the purity of the feeling I had momentarily experienced. I was instantly reminded of the emotions I had felt upon catching sight of Sonoko that morning of March the ninth. It was exactly the same now; it was the same thing. It was the same even to the feeling of sorrow that seemed to have pierced me to the heart.

This little incident became an unforgettable thing, giving rise during the next few days to a vivid tumult of excitement within me. Surely it can't be true that I'm still in love with Sonoko, surely I'm incapable of loving a woman—until the day before these beliefs had been my only trusty and obedient followers, of whose loyalty I had felt absolutely assured, and yet now even they were in mutiny against me.

In this way my memories suddenly regained their power over me; it was a *coup d'état* that took the form of pure agony. "Trivial" memories which I should have cleaned up tidily and thrown away two years before had now grown strangely large and been restored to life before my very eyes—just like a bastard child who has been forgotten and then suddenly turns up, full grown. These memories were tinged neither with that air of "sweet sentiment" which I had invented on those several occasions, nor with that businesslike air which I had later used for disposing of them: instead, they were permeated throughout with a single, palpable air of torment. If my feeling had been one of remorse, I could have found a way of enduring it, simply by following the path already well blazed by countless forerunners. But my pain was a strangely clear-cut agony, not fuzzy remorse; it was like being forced to look down from a window at a reflection of fierce summer sunlight that is dividing the street into a glaring contrast of sun and shadow.

One cloudy afternoon during the rainy season I happened to be walking through Azabu on an errand. This was a section of the city I had seldom been in. Suddenly, from behind me, someone called my name. It was Sonoko. Upon looking around and catching sight of her I was not as surprised as I had been that time on the streetcar when I had mistaken another girl for her. To me this chance encounter seemed perfectly natural, as though I had foreseen it all along. I felt as though I had known everything about this instant since long before.

She was wearing a simple dress, with a flower pattern like that of chic wallpaper, and no ornament other than some lace at the V of the neck; there was nothing about her to proclaim that she was now a married woman. She was probably returning from drawing rations as she was carrying a bucket and was also followed by an old servant woman carrying another bucket. She sent the woman on home and walked along talking with me.

"You've become a little thin, haven't you?"

"Ah, thanks to studying for the exams."

"So? Please take care of your health."

Then we fell silent for a time. Soft sunlight began

pouring into the quiet residential street, which had escaped the bombing. A wet duck waddled out from a kitchen doorway and went quacking along the gutter before us. I felt happy.

"What are you reading these days?" I asked.

"Novels you mean? Well, I've read Tanizaki's *Some Prefer Nettles,* and then—"

I broke in. "You haven't read ———?" I said, naming a novel then in vogue.

"That one with the naked woman?" she said.

"Huh?" I said, surprised.

"It's disgusting—that picture on the cover."

Two years before she would never have been able to look one in the face and say "naked woman." The mere fact that she had used these words, trivial though they were, brought with it a painfully clear realization that Sonoko was no longer the virginal girl I had known.

She came to a halt as we reached a corner and said:

"This where I turn off. My house is at the end of this street."

Feeling a pain at the thought of parting from her, I lowered my eyes and looked at the bucket in her hand. It was filled with *konnyaku,* a jostling, gelatinous mass bathed in sunlight, looking like a woman's skin tanned by the sun at the seashore.

"*Konnyaku* will spoil beyond eating if you leave it in the sun too long," I said.

"That's right," Sonoko answered in a loud joking voice. "It's a big responsibility."

"Well, good-bye."

"Yes, good luck." She began walking away.

I called her back and asked if she ever went to visit her family. She replied easily that she happened to be going there the following Saturday.

Then we parted, and for the first time I noticed an important thing—today it seemed as though she had forgiven me. Why had she forgiven me? Could there be any greater insult than such magnanimity? But maybe, I told myself, my pain might be healed if I were to be clearly insulted by her just once more.

Saturday seemed long in coming. Kusano was attending the university in Kyoto, but as luck would have it he was home for a visit. Saturday afternoon I went to see him.

As we were talking I heard a sound that made me doubt my own ears. It was the sound of a piano. The playing was no longer immature, but full bodied, full of reverberations that seemed to flow and spread freely, replete, sparkling.

"Who's that playing?" I asked.

"It's Sonoko. She's visiting here today," Kusano answered, knowing nothing.

With a painful flash, all the old memories came back, one by one.

I was depressed by the fact that, out of his good will for me, Kusano had never said a word about my indirect refusal of Sonoko. I wanted some proof that she had been at least slightly hurt at that time; I wanted to discover some unhappiness in her corresponding to my own. But once again "time" had intervened, growing as rank as weeds between Kusano and Sonoko and myself, and any frank expression of feelings, uncolored by pride or vanity or prudence, had become impossible for us.

The piano stopped. Kusano had the wit to ask if he should get her to join us. He went out and soon returned with her. The three of us started gossiping, with much meaningless laughter, about acquaintances at the Foreign Office, where Sonoko's husband was working.

Presently Kusano's mother called him and he went to her. Sonoko and I were left alone in the room together, just as we had been on that day two years earlier.

Sonoko told me with no little childish pride how it had been her husband's efforts that had saved the Kusano house from requisitioning by the Occupation Forces. From the beginning I had always found her boastfulness attractive. An overly modest woman is without charm, as is a haughty woman also, and there was an innocent, likeable quality of womanliness about Sonoko's quiet and restrained bragging.

"By the way," she said, still speaking quietly, "there's something I've been wanting and wanting to ask you but haven't been able to ask before. I've kept wondering why we didn't marry. After I got the answer that you sent my brother I simply couldn't understand anything at all about the world. Every day I did nothing but wonder and wonder. Even yet I can't understand why we couldn't have married. . . ."

She turned her face away from me slightly, with an appearance of anger, showing her slightly blushing cheeks, and then went on speaking as though reading aloud:

"Was it because you disliked me?"

Her question sounded as straightforward as a simple business inquiry, and my heart responded to it with a sort of violent and pathetic joy. Then in a flash this vicious joy turned into pain. It was a truly subtle pain. A certain amount of the pain was genuine, but beyond this there was also the agony of hurt pride at discovering that the revival of the "trivial" events of two years before could make my heart ache so. I had wanted to be liberated from her. But I found it as impossible as ever.

"You still don't know anything at all about the world," I told her. "That's one of your good points, your ignorance of worldly things. But listen, the world is not made just so two people who are in love can always get married. That's exactly what I wrote your brother. Besides"—I felt that I was about to say a womanish thing and wanted to shut up, but could not stop—"besides, nowhere in that letter did I say definitely that marriage was out of the question. As I said, it was only because I was not yet twenty-one, and was still a student, and it was too sudden. And then while I was hesitating you went and got married in such a hurry."

"Well, as for me, I have no reason to regret it. My husband loves me and I also love him. I'm truly happy. There's nothing more I could ask for. And yet—maybe it's bad to think so, but sometimes—I wonder what's the best way to say it—Sometimes in my imagination I see another me leading a different life. Then I become confused and feel I'm about to say something I oughtn't say. I feel I'm about to think something I oughtn't think, and become so upset I can't stand it. My husband is a great help at such times. He treats me gently, just like a child."

"It may sound conceited, but shall I ll you what I think? At those times you're hating me. You're hating me violently."

Sonoko did not even know the meaning of hating. Gently, seriously, she pretended to pout and said:

"You're welcome to think whatever you like."

"Can't we meet once more, just we two alone?" Abruptly, I found myself pleading with her as though something were rushing me onward. "There wouldn't be anything to be ashamed of. I'd be satisfied just to look at your face. I no longer have a right to say anything. Even if you don't say a word it'll be all right. Even only thirty minutes will be all right."

"Then what would be the use of meeting? And anyway, if we met once, wouldn't you just say let's meet again? At my house my mother-in-law is strict and every time I go out she even asks where I'm going and when I'll be back. To meet with such uncomfortable feelings—but if—" Her speech faltered an instant. "Well, there's something called the human heart, and no one knows what makes it beat."

"That's right. But you're as much a Miss Dainty as ever, aren't you? Why can't you think about things more cheerfully and casually?" (What lies I was telling!)

"That's all right for a man. But not for a married woman. You'll understand all right when you have a wife. I don't think it's possible to be too careful about such things."

"Now you're sounding like somebody's elder sister giving advice. . . ."

Just then Kusano returned and our conversation was broken off.

Even during our conversation my mind had been filled with an endless swarm of doubts. I swore by God that my mood of wanting to meet Sonoko was a genuine one. But in it there was clearly not the slightest sexual desire. So then, what kind of desire was it that made me want to meet her so? Might it not be only self-deception again, this passion that so obviously was not sexual desire? In the first place, can there be such a thing as love that has no basis whatsoever in sexual desire? Isn't that a clear and obvious absurdity?

But then another thought occurred to me: if we

grant that human passion has the power to rise above all absurdity, how can it be argued that it does not have the power to rise above the absurdities of passion itself?

Since that decisive night I had cleverly managed to avoid women. Since that night I had not touched the lips of a single woman—much less the ephebic lips that so genuinely called to my desire—not even if I found myself in a situation in which it was rude not to do so. . . . So then, the advent of summer threatened my solitude even more than the spring had done. And full summer lashed the galloping horses of my sexual desire. It consumed and tortured my flesh. To endure it I had to resort to my bad habit sometimes as much as five times in one day.

My ignorance had been enlightened by reading the theories of Hirschfeld, who explains inversion as a perfectly simple biological phenomenon. I realized now that even that decisive night had been a natural consequence and that there was no cause for shame. My imaginative lust for the ephebe, although never once turning to pederasty, had taken a well-defined form, which the investigators have shown to be almost equally prevalent. It is said that the same impulse as this I was feeling is not uncommon among Germans. The diary of Count von Platen provides a most representative example. Winckelmann also was the same. And, turning to Renaissance Italy, it is clear that Michelangelo was the possessor of impulses in the same category as mine.

But this does not mean that my emotional life was set to rights by my intellectual understanding of these scientific theories. It was difficult for inversion to become an actuality in my case simply because in me the impulse went no further than sexuality, went no further than being a dark impulse crying out in vain, struggling helplessly, blindly. Even the excitement aroused in me by an attractive ephebe stopped short at mere sexual desire. To give a superficial explanation, my soul still belonged to Sonoko. Although it does not mean that I accept the concept outright, I can conveniently use the medieval diagram of the struggle between soul and body to make my meaning clear: in me there was a cleavage, pure and simple, between spirit and flesh. To me Sonoko appeared the incarnation of my love of normality itself, my love of things of the spirit, my love of everlasting things.

But such a simple explanation does not dispose of the problem. The emotions have no liking for fixed order. Instead, like tiny particles in the ether, they fly about freely, float haphazardly, and prefer to be forever wavering. . . .

A year passed before Sonoko and I awakened. I had been successful in the civil-service examinations, graduated from the university, and had an administrative job in one of the ministries. During that year we managed to meet several times, now as though by chance, now under the pretext of some trivial business, but only every two or three months and even then only for a daylight hour or so—meeting without anything happening, and parting the same way. That was all. No one could have censured my behavior. Nor did Sonoko venture beyond trifling reminiscences or conversations making modest fun of our present situation. Our connection could never have been called an intrigue, and one would even have hesitated to call it a relationship. Even when we met we would be thinking of nothing but how to make each parting a clean-cut break.

I was satisfied with this. More than that, I was thankful to something for the mystic richness of this desultory relationship. There was not a day in which I did not think of Sonoko, and each time we met I experienced a tranquil happiness. It seemed as though the delicate tension and pure symmetry of our rendezvous extended to every corner of my life and imposed on it a clear though exceedingly fragile discipline.

But a year passed and we awakened. We discovered that we were living in a nursery no longer but were inhabitants of an adult edifice where any door that opened only part way had to be repaired promptly. Our relationship was just such a door, one that could never be opened beyond a certain point, and it was sure to require repairing sooner or later. Beyond this there was also the fact that adults cannot endure the monotonous games that delight children. The many meetings which we examined one by one were nothing but stereotyped things, each of like size and thickness—a pack of playing cards whose edges matched to a fraction of an inch when stacked one above the other.

Moreover, from this relationship I was cunningly extracting an immoral delight, which only I could understand. My immorality was a subtle one, going even a step beyond the ordinary vices of the world, and like an exquisite poison, it was pure corruption. Since immorality was the very basis and first principle of my nature I found an all the more truly fiendish flavor of secret sin in my virtuous behavior, in this blameless relationship with a woman, in my honorable conduct, and in being regarded as a man of lofty principles.

We had stretched out our arms to each other and supported something in our joined hands, but this thing we were holding was like a sort of gas that exists when you believe in its existence and disappears when you doubt. The task of supporting it seems simple at first glance, but actually requires an ultimate refinement of calculation and a consummate skill. I had called an artificial "normality" into being in that space within our hands, and had induced Sonoko to take part in the dangerous operation of trying to sustain an almost chimerical "love" from moment to moment. She seemed to have become party to the plot without realizing it. This lack of realization on her part was probably the only reason her assistance was so effective.

But the time came when even Sonoko became dimly aware of the indomitable force of this nameless danger, this danger that differed completely from the usual roughhewn dangers of the world in having a precise, measurable density.

One day in late summer I met Sonoko, who had just returned from a mountain resort, at a restaurant called the Coq d'Or. As soon as we met I told her about my having resigned from the civil service.

"What'll you do now?"

"Oh, let the future take care of itself."

"Well, it is a surprise." She did not have anything else to say about the matter. This sort of etiquette of non-interference was already well established between us.

Sonoko had been tanned by the mountain sun, and her skin had lost its radiant whiteness there above her breasts. The large pearl in her ring had become gloomily clouded from the heat. The sound of her high voice, always a blend of sadness and indolence, was most appropriate to the season.

For a time we again carried on a meaningless, endlessly revolving, insincere conversation. At times it seemed nothing but a great skidding through empty air. It gave us a feeling that we were overhearing a conversation being carried on by two strangers. It was a feeling like that felt at the borderline between sleeping and waking, when one's impatient efforts to go back to sleep without awakening from a happy dream only make the recapture of the dream all the more impossible. I discovered how our hearts, as though infected with some malignant virus, were being eaten away by the uneasy awakening that was brazenly intruding upon our dream, by the futile pleasure of our dream seen at the threshold of consciousness. As though at a signal previously agreed upon, the disease had attacked both our hearts almost simultaneously. We reacted with a show of gaiety. As though each of us feared what the other might say at any moment, we capped joke upon joke.

Even though her sun tan introduced a tiny note of discord, there beneath her fashionable upswept coiffure the same tranquillity as always was overflowing from her softly moist eyes, her youthful eyebrows, her slightly heavyish lips. Whenever other women passed our table they always noticed Sonoko. A waiter was moving about the room, carrying a silver tray on which iced desserts were arranged on a large block of ice carved in the shape of a swan. Sonoko was softly jingling the clasp of her plastic handbag, and a ring glittered on her finger.

"Are you bored with this?" I asked.

"Don't say that."

Her tone of voice sounded full of a weariness that was somehow strange. It could even have been called charming. She had turned her head and was looking out the window at the summer street. When she spoke again her words came slowly:

"Sometimes I become confused. I wonder why we're meeting like this. And yet in the end I always meet you again."

"Probably because at least it's not a meaningless minus. Even if it certainly is a meaningless plus."

"But I have something called a husband, remember. Even if the plus is meaningless, there oughtn't to be room for any plus at all."

"It's tiresome arithmetic, isn't it?"

I perceived that Sonoko had finally arrived at the doorway to doubt. She had begun to feel that the door that opened only halfway could not be left as it was. Perhaps by now this sort of sensitivity to disorder had come to absorb the largest part of the feelings Sonoko and I shared in common. I too was still far from the age when one is willing to accept things the way they are.

And yet it seemed as though I had suddenly been confronted with clear proof that my nameless fear had infected Sonoko unawares and, moreover, that the sole possession we shared in common was the sign of fear. Sonoko again gave voice to this fear. I tried not to listen. But my mouth made flippant replies.

"If we go on like this," she said, "what do you think will happen? Won't we be driven into some corner we can't escape from?"

"I think that I respect you and that there's nothing to be ashamed of before anybody. Why is it wrong for two friends to meet?"

"That's the way it's been up to now. It's been just like you say. I think you've acted very honorably. But I don't know about the future. Even though we don't do the slightest thing to be ashamed of, I still somehow have terrible dreams. Then I feel as though God is punishing me for future sins."

The solid sound of this word future made me shudder.

"If we keep on like this," she continued, "I'm afraid that one day something will happen that will hurt us both. And after we're hurt won't it be too late? Because isn't what we're doing the same as playing with fire?"

"What kind of thing do you mean when you say playing with fire?"

"Oh, all sorts of things."

"But you can't regard what we're doing as playing with fire. It's just like playing with water."

She did not smile. During the occasional pauses in our conversation she had been pressing her lips together fiercely.

"Lately I've begun to think I'm an awful woman. I can't think of myself as anything but a bad woman with a filthy soul. Even in my dreams I oughtn't think about anyone except my husband. I've made up my mind to be baptized this fall."

I guessed that in this idle sort of confession, due partly to an intoxication with the sound of her own words, Sonoko was approaching the feminine paradox of meaning the opposite of what she said and was unconsciously wanting to say what must not be said. As for me, I had the right neither to rejoice at this nor to lament it. In the first place, how could I, who felt not the slightest jealousy of her husband, have exercised these rights either by claiming or refusing them? I was silent. The sight of my own hands, white and frail at the height of summer, filled me with despair.

"And right now?" I said at last.

"Now?" She lowered her eyes.

"Yes, who is it you're thinking about right now?"

". . . My husband."

"Then it's not necessary to be baptized, is it?"

"Oh, it is! . . . I'm afraid. I still feel as though I am shaking violently."

"So then, right now?"

"Now?"

Sonoko lifted her grave eyes as though unconsciously asking someone for help. In the pupils of her eyes I discovered a beauty I had never seen before. They were deep, unblinking, fatalistic pupils, like fountains constantly singing with an outpouring of emotions. I was at a loss for words, as was always the case when she turned those eyes upon me. Suddenly I reached to the ashtray across the table and ground out my half-smoked cigarette. As I did so the slender vase in the center of the table upset, soaking the table with water.

A waiter came and cleaned up the mess. The sight of the water-wrinkled tablecloth being wiped gave us a wretched feeling, providing us with an excuse for leaving a little earlier.

The summer streets were annoyingly crowded. Healthy looking lovers were passing by, their chests thrown out, their arms bare. I felt that every one of them was scorning me. The scorn was like the strong summer sunlight burning into me.

Thirty minutes remained before time for us to part. I cannot say whether it was precisely because of the pain of parting, but a gloomy, nervous irritation resembling a sort of passion had given rise to a feeling of wanting to daub that half-hour over with thick colors like oil paints. I halted in front of a dance hall where a loud-speaker was hurling the wild strains of a rhumba into the street. I had suddenly been reminded of a line from a poem I had read long before:

. . . But always it was a dance without an end. . . .

I had forgotten the rest. It must be from a poem by André Salmon. . . .

Although such a place was outside her experience, Sonoko nodded assent and accompanied me into the dance hall for thirty minutes of dancing.

The hall was crowded with office workers who came every day for an hour or two of dancing, extending their lunch hours to suit their own pleasure. A sultry heat struck us full in the face. Abetted by a defective ventilation system and heavy drapes that shut out the open air, the stifling fever-heat that stagnated within the place was raising a milky fog of dust-motes against the reflecting lights. One did not need to be told what kind of people these were who were dancing there, not noticing the heat, effusing smells of sweat and bad perfume and cheap pomade. I was sorry I had brought Sonoko.

But it was too late to turn back now. Without any heart for it, we pushed through the dancing crowd. Even the infrequent electric fans did not deliver the slightest breeze. Young fellows were dancing with the hostesses, cheek pressed against sweaty cheek. The sides of the girls' noses had become murky, and their sweat-caked face powder looked like acne upon their skin. The backs of their dresses looked even more soiled and sodden than the tablecloth had looked a little while before. Whether one danced or not, sweat spread over the body. Sonoko was taking short breaths as though suffocating.

Looking for a breath of fresh air, we passed through an archway entwined with artificial, out-of-season flowers, went out into the courtyard, and seated ourselves on two of the crude chairs. Here there was fresh air, true enough, but the concrete floor was reflecting heat intense enough to reach even to the chairs in the shade. Our mouths were sticky with the syrupy sweetness of Coca-Cola. It seemed that Sonoko too had been silenced by the same agony of disdain I was feeling about everything. After a time I could no longer endure this silence and began looking around us.

There was a fat girl leaning lazily against the wall, fanning her bosom with her handkerchief. The swing band was playing a quickstep that seemed overpowering. There in the courtyard were some potted evergreens that rose askew from the parched earth in which they were confined. All the chairs in the shade of the awning were taken, no one wishing to brave the sunlight.

There was a single group, however, sitting there full in the sunshine, chatting together as though they were completely alone. It was made up of two girls and two young men. One of the girls was smoking a cigarette in an affected way that showed she was unaccustomed to smoking, giving a little choking cough after each puff. Both of the girls were wearing peculiar dresses that seemed to have been made from summer-kimono material. The dresses were sleeveless, revealing arms as red as those of fishwives, marked here and there with insect bites. Every time the boys made a coarse joke the girls would look at each other and laugh simperingly. The fierce summer sun that beat down on their heads did not seem to bother them particularly.

One of the boys was wearing an aloha shirt, a garment then much in vogue among the gangs of young toughs in the city. His face was pale and crafty looking, but he had powerful arms. A lewd smile was forever flickering about his lips, appearing and disappearing. He would make the girls laugh by poking their breasts with a finger.

Then my attention was drawn to the other boy. He was a youth of twenty-one or -two, with coarse but regular and swarthy features. He had taken off his shirt and stood there half naked, rewinding a belly-band about his middle. The coarse cotton material was soaked with sweat and had become a light-gray color. He seemed to be intentionally dawdling over his task of winding and was constantly joining in the talk and laughter of his companions. His naked chest showed bulging muscles, fully developed and tensely knit; a deep cleft ran down between the solid muscles of his chest toward his abdomen. The thick, fetter-like sinews of his flesh narrowed down from different directions to the sides of his chest, where they interlocked in tight coils. The hot mass of his smooth torso was being severely and tightly imprisoned by each succeeding turn of the soiled cotton belly-band. His bare, sun-tanned shoulders gleamed as though covered with oil. And black tufts stuck out from the cracks of his armpits, catching the sunlight, curling and glittering with glints of gold.

At this sight, above all at the sight of the peony tattooed on his hard chest, I was beset by sexual desire. My fervent gaze was fixed upon that rough and savage, but incomparably beautiful, body. Its owner was laughing there under the sun. When he threw back his head I could see his thick, muscular neck. A strange shudder ran through my innermost heart. I could no longer take my eyes off him.

I had forgotten Sonoko's existence. I was thinking of but one thing: Of his going out onto the streets of high summer just as he was, half-naked, and getting into a fight with a rival gang. Of a sharp dagger cutting through that belly-band, piercing that torso. Of that soiled belly-band beautifully dyed with blood. Of his gory corpse being put on an improvised stretcher, made of a window shutter, and brought back here. . . .

"There's just five minutes left." Sonoko's high, sad voice reached my ears. I turned to her wonderingly.

At this instant something inside of me was torn in two with brutal force. It was as though a thunderbolt had fallen and cleaved asunder a living tree. I heard the structure, which I had been building piece by piece with all my might up to now, collapse miserably to the ground. I felt as though I had witnessed the instant in which my existence had been turned into some sort of fearful non-being. I closed my eyes and after an instant regained a hold on my icy-cold sense of duty.

"Only five minutes? It was wrong to bring you to such a place. Are you angry? A person like you oughtn't see the vulgarity of such low people. I've heard that this dance hall doesn't have the knack of buying off these gangs of hoodlums and that they've started forcing their way in to dance free no matter how much they're refused."

But I was the only one who had been looking at them. Sonoko had not noticed them. She had been trained not to see things that should not be seen. She had simply kept her eyes fixed absent-mindedly on the sweaty row of backs that stood watching the dancing.

But even so, it seemed that the atmosphere of the place had worked some sort of chemical change in Sonoko's heart as well, without her being aware of it. Presently something like a token of a smile appeared on her bashful lips, as though she were enjoying in advance what she was about to say:

"It's a funny thing to ask, but you already *have,* haven't you? Of course you've already done *that,* haven't you?"

I was completely exhausted. And yet some hair trigger

was still set in my mind, making me give a plausible answer quicker than thought.

"Umm . . . I already have, I'm sorry to say."

"When?"

"Last spring."

"With whom?"

I was amazed at the mixture of naïveté and sophistication in her question. She was incapable of imagining me in connection with a girl whose name she would not know.

"I can't tell you her name."

"Come, who was she?"

"Please don't ask me."

Perhaps because she heard the too-naked tone of entreaty behind my words, she instantly fell silent, as though frightened. I was making every possible effort to keep her from noticing how the blood was draining from my face. The moment for parting stood waiting eagerly. A vulgar blues was being kneaded into time. We were caught up motionless within the sound of the sentimental voice issuing from the loud-speaker.

Sonoko and I looked at our wrist watches almost at the same instant. . . .

It was time. As I got up, I stole one more glance toward those chairs in the sun. The group had apparently gone to dance, and the chairs stood empty in the blazing sunshine. Some sort of beverage had been spilled on the table top and was throwing back glittering, threatening reflections.